Death On The Hill

A Novel By
James Snedden

Published By
Barclay Books, LLC

St. Petersburg, Florida

PUBLISHED BY BARCLAY BOOKS, LLC
6161 51st Street South
St. Petersburg, Florida 33715
www.barclaybooks.com

Printed and bound in the United States of America

ISBN: 1-931402-05-1

To Beth, my wife, my collaborator, my editor in residence, and my staunchest supporter. Thank you for your understanding, help, and patience.

PROLOGUE

Shivering in the coastal evening chill, his gloved hand felt for the handle of the knife tucked in the belt of his jumpsuit.

Framed by the window he was peering through, an attractive Asian woman, with a poodle at her feet, watched television. At the conclusion of the show, she got up, moved toward a hall closet, and got out her windbreaker, momentarily blocking his view. Instinctively, he drew back, crouching lower in the bushes as she emerged from the side door of the house.

It wasn't until he spotted the leash-less poodle running down the driveway toward the street, streaking past the bushes without sniffing them, as it charged to its favorite shrub twenty feet away, that his gloved hand quickly pulled out the knife.

With the knife ready to strike, he remained motionless, his eyes following the woman as she made her way cautiously down the three steps to the driveway.

Suddenly, as lights of an oncoming car turned onto the usually deserted street, the woman began running, calling the dog's name. Shortly, thereafter, headlights of a second car, from the other direction, appeared, heading toward the house.

He dropped to the ground, face down, behind the bushes while the garage door opened. It was only a matter of seconds before the car pulled into the driveway and the garage door once again closed.

Rising up on one knee, he peered through the cracks in the bushes, observing the woman at the foot of the driveway. Again, he froze, not making a sound.

Lights appeared in an upstairs window as the barking dog ran past the bushes, to the foot of the steps leading to the front door of the house. The woman followed closely behind, calling for the animal to be quiet.

With each of her approaching strides, his grip on the knife handle became tighter. When she was four steps away, he sprang from his hiding place. Like a trained athlete, his next motion was automatic. His victim was so intent on the dog that she never saw him coming from the bushes. One hand reached out in front of her, stopping her progress and stifling any outcry, while the other reached around, cleanly slitting her throat. She was dead before he dropped her body.

Quickly, he stepped over her, avoiding the blood gushing from her severed throat, as he reached for the cowering poodle that met the same fate as its mistress.

After cutting an ear off of the dog, and another from the woman, he deposited them in a plastic sandwich bag he had removed from his jumpsuit pocket. Then he disappeared into the darkness.

CHAPTER ONE

I suppose it was just a coincidence that my former college roommate called when he did. I was planning an extended leave of absence from my job as an investigative reporter for the *Chicago Tribune*.

Bill had recently purchased a semi-weekly newspaper in Palos Verdes Estates in Southern California where he had grown up, and wanted me to take a look at his new "baby." Had I known what was in store for me, I might not have been so quick to jump on his offer for a free vacation.

On the second night of my stay in Bill's condo, I was awakened by the touch of a hand on my sunburned back.

"Jeremy, get up," Bill said. There's been a murder in Montemalaga, and we have to get there fast."

As he peeled the covers off my baked body, I regretted my day on the beach. "Who the hell cares about a murder in Spain."

"Montemalaga is here on the hill. If we hurry, we can get pictures the other newspapers won't have."

Once a reporter, always a reporter. I scrambled into a tee shirt, shorts, and tennis shoes, while Bill retrieved the car from the garage.

As we sped toward the crime scene, in an attempt to take my mind off of the way Bill was driving, I asked him for details, starting with how he had found out about the murder if the larger papers, like the *Los Angeles Times*, for example, hadn't. In his over simplistic manner he told me that the wife of the on-call detective had telephoned him.

"You were never one to infringe on someone else's territory, so why would she call you?

He laughed at my question. "She majored in journalism at UCLA, and now that the kids are in school she wants to get back to work. She does freelance stuff for me. Oh," he added as an afterthought, "we went to PV high together back in the old days."

"That explains everything." I remarked sarcastically. "But if the success of a weekly paper on the Palos Verdes Peninsula relies on homicides you might be in trouble, my friend."

"Local news is local news and that's what we rely on to sell papers. People subscribe to get an in-depth view of what's going on locally, and death on the hill is as local as you get.

"Besides, it's a good diversion from covering the sorority dinners where the girls, and I use that word loosely, call a press conference to announce they are donating money to a local arts group, and then find out it's a fifty dollar check."

"Oh, come on," I said. "It can't be all that bad."

"Oh, but it is. Right after I took the paper over, this local sorority that was presenting a touring theatrical group with a check, called us. A photographer and I went over and found out the high flyers gave the princely sum of fifty bucks. To make matters worse, they weren't even photogenic."

"You are terrible," I said. "And you tell me to be less caustic."

"I guess it comes with the territory."

"Yeah," I said. But I can get away with it, friend.

When I get too sarcastic, I have an editor who'll tone the piece down. You don't have that luxury and could bite the hand that feeds you."

We pulled into the street where the crime took place. It wasn't difficult to find the house. There were enough police cars, floodlights and ambulances there to mistake it for a doughnut shop. After parking several houses away and showing our press passes—Bill's from his paper and mine from the *Trib*, which didn't even raise an eyebrow from the patrolperson—we found out that Bill had been wrong. Not only was the local *South Bay Breeze* there, but the *Los Angeles Times* was also represented.

I couldn't resist. "Looks like the little woman does a lot of moonlighting."

Bill mumbled incoherently as I followed him up the driveway. He started taking pictures while I nosed around. A detective soon stopped me. I knew he was a detective because of the badge hanging from his windbreaker. Not only that, he was a Palos Verdes Estates detective, so I found myself standing face to face with the husband of the biggest mouth in town.

"I don't believe I've seen you around before. I'm Detective Rodney Bilbo of the PV Estates police department. Who are you and what paper are you from?"

"Jeremy Dawkins. The *Chicago Trib*."

"The *Chicago Trib*?" he said with the look of a person who was having his leg pulled and didn't like it. "What in the hell is the *Chicago Trib* doing here? What did you do?

lease a Concorde?"

I knew we were going to get along fine. When I told him I was on vacation visiting Bill, he mellowed and told me what had gone on that night.

The dead person was an Asian woman in her late thirties. She had been home alone. Her husband was an airline pilot. She had been out walking her dog, a toy poodle, when the assailant had come up from behind, slitting her throat with a knife. From the body indentations in the bushes by the side of the driveway, the killer had been waiting for some time. In fact, at one point he had lain prone on the ground.

"So the killer must have known that she walked the dog at night and waited for her?"

"That's what it looks like, so far," said Bilbo.

"Who found the body?"

"The husband. He came home, parked his car in the garage, went upstairs and changed out of his uniform, and then came down to meet his wife. When he couldn't find her in the house, he went outside to look for her, assuming she was walking the dog. That's when he found her and the poodle lying on the driveway. He then called 911."

"So, if the husband found the body on the driveway, the killer must have killed the wife when the husband was upstairs. Otherwise, he would have seen the body when he drove up."

"Right. He obviously knew the pattern."

I interrupted. "Which means that he had either cased the situation before, or some third party told him. Do you have any suspects?"

"We've already checked the husband's story. He just flew in from Hong Kong. That's about all I can tell you now. We'll know more after we have a chance to go over the crime scene in more detail and after the coroner does his thing."

"I'll be in touch."

"I'm sure you will," said Bilbo."

It took me a half hour, but I finally succeeded in convincing Bill that (a) he didn't have a scoop, and (b) it would be better to give Detective Bilbo some time to sort things out. Then write an in-depth, follow-up story after the *Times* and the *Breeze* had gone on to bigger and better things.

I even volunteered to write it. That was my first … no … second mistake. My first was letting Bill get me out of bed to come to the crime scene in the first place.

CHAPTER TWO

The next morning I woke up hungry.

Like myself, Bill is divorced. I knew what to expect for breakfast. There is nothing more pathetic than the refrigerator of a divorced male in his mid-forties, and Bill was no exception. To make matters worse, he was a health freak living on chicken breasts and raw veggies.

When Bill gave up social events like romantic dinners in good restaurants because they fried too many things, and bike riding became a priority, his marriage died.

Although I've been trying to cut down on my fat intake, I haven't gone off the deep end like Bill. Maybe it's because I still live in the Midwest and haven't succumbed to the lure of Southern California where overreaction takes on religious significance. I still like a good filet mignon, and I continue to be faithful to the Brewmeisters in St. Louis and Milwaukee who rarely let me down.

I managed to find some skim milk behind two containers of bottled water. The cabinet next to the fridge yielded a piece of whole wheat bread, which I had to eat without butter.

The drive from Bill's condo to the paper took seven minutes, which was only three minutes longer than it took us to walk from the condo to the garage. Now, that is disgusting. No one should have only a seven-minute drive to work. It's un-American, to say the least.

Bill was the first to arrive and, therefore, unlock the door. That, too, was foreign to me—a locked door to a newspaper. After entering, the first thing he did was listen to his answering machine. He had four or five messages. I'm really not sure because I stopped listening after the first. It was from one of his part-time reporters informing him to be sure and pick-up the *Daily Breeze* because there had been a murder in PV Estates that night.

At most newspapers, the first thing people do when they get to work is head for the coffee. On a weekly newspaper where the owner/editor/copywriter/advertising salesperson is a health nut, the first thing to come out of the refrigerator is a bottle of water. My host handed me one. I asked him if he wanted me to water the plants. He ignored me and sat down behind the desk. I found out later that I was supposed to suck on the water bottle at polite intervals.

Bill's office didn't look like a newspaperman's. His desk was neat—not at all like the editors I was used to— and he actually had things in files. The amazing thing was that he kept it this way without a full time secretary.

Sitting at his desk while I was still standing, Bill gave me the most serious look he could muster. A more prudent person would have made some lame excuse to leave, check into a local motel and get on with their vacation. But I have never been called prudent. Besides, old friendships can't be written off because of some slight inconvenience. One takes too long to cultivate, and they are too difficult to replace.

He pointed to one of the chairs in the office before

buttering me up with, "You're one of the best investigative reporters in the business." Then he said, "By my reckoning, this case won't be solved quickly. Both the *Times* and the *Breeze* will soon lose interest. They've got more than just Peninsula readership to satisfy. My paper, on the other hand, devotes one hundred percent of its coverage to local news, so my readers have a longer attention span."

The more Bill talked, the more excited he became. I can't remember seeing him so animated. His arms were flaying around like an Italian cook after being told his meatballs tasted like McDonald's hamburger.

"If every week the *Digest* can have something new, regardless of size," he continued, "I'll pick up subscribers. More importantly, if the *Digest* can crack the case before the police, it can even be in line for a Pulitzer. So, if you would nose around and see what you can come up with. You know. At least for the time you're going to stay. Who knows what might happen."

I got completely caught up by Bill's enthusiasm. I didn't argue with him that I was a better than average bear at investigative reporting. But I did point out what he well knew—that behind every great news hound are his sources, and I had none in Southern California.

"I don't have a source," I said, "in the local police department to feed me information. I don't have ears on the streets to pick up the news on that channel. And, most of all, I still can't find my way to Torrance without stopping to ask directions." For fear of bursting his balloon and breaking his fragile heart, however, I didn't mention that I also didn't have the prestige of a *Times* or *Tribune* behind me here to open doors.

That's when he pulled out his trump card. "Remember when we almost got caught in the panty raid at school?   I saved your bacon and kept you from getting expelled because I was banging the housemother. If it wasn't for me, you would have been thrown out of school and wouldn't even have a career." I knew he must be desperate to have dug that far back in the memory bank.

"All right," I said. "This'll wipe the slate clean for those sacrifices. I'll agree to work on this case, but no more than three hours a day. Got that? And, in return, you smooth the way for me with the good detective, Rodney Bilbo …"

The last word was still somewhere between my lips and Bill's ears when he picked up the telephone and punched in the number of the Palos Verdes Estates Police Department. It was then that I realized the similarities between a large city like Chicago and a small town like PV Estates. They are the same when it comes to one thing— voice mail.

I listened to Bill leave his message for the detective before he turned his attention back to me and said,

"He'll get back to me. What angle do you want to start from?"

The office wasn't large enough to pace in, but I gave it my best shot. "Don't get too antsy," I reminded him. "First, I have to find out everything they know about the victim and the victim's husband." We both knew that the spouse is always the prime suspect.

It was Bill's turn to pace. "Based on the husband's reaction, he's either a good actor or he's not guilty."

"I disagree. It's one thing to put a hit out on your wife, but quite another to see her dead body lying on the ground in a pool of blood. I've seen spouses go to pieces with the murder weapons in their hands when they see what they've done. No, the real thing is a little more unnerving in real time than on the tube or the big screen."

Bill led me to a small office cubicle I could call my own. Now he could pace in his own office without interruption as he worried about what else he was going to put into the paper besides the murder. I settled down to plan my method of getting Bill's scoop.

The fact that I didn't have good sources in California wouldn't stop me from finding out some things about the lady in question. Bill had given me her name and, as soon as I found out her maiden name, I could make a few calls back to Chicago and have a make run on her through the Feds. There was also plenty of public record information for me to investigate. After all, that's why there's the word "investigative" before "reporter" in our job descriptions.

Investigative reporting is like good police work. You start digging and asking questions to see where they lead. The key is to ask the right questions and follow the right leads, then separate the truth from the fiction. Everyone has a theory, and most want to share it with you, particularly if there might be a chance to get their names in print. Every reporter has his or her own methods. Many of my colleagues use brainstorming, but I prefer the starbursting technique. Brainstorming allows the mind to flow freely from thought to thought with each one stimulating others. Starbursting focuses on a topic and flows outward. It begins by asking, "What are the questions?"

I wrote the first question: "Why an Asian?" Then, "Why this particular Asian woman?" It didn't take long before I had two pages of questions.

I moved to the second part of my ritual. I attempted to organize the questions and place them in logical groups.

First, was the word "ethnic." Next, came "instrument." From this cluster came the questions, "Why a knife?" "Why not a simple drive-by shooting?" "Why not a shotgun?" After all, it was dark and deserted in that part of town, and one blast of a shotgun would have done the job. There probably would have been less risk of detection than waiting in the bushes half the night. The person could have been out and gone before the neighbors had the chance to turn on their lights.

My last cluster was "people." This provided me with the most provocative questions, the obvious being, "Who uses knives?" followed by, "Why do killers use knives?"

I was soon totally absorbed in the subject and started getting ahead of myself, formulating a series of syllogisms. The first one I wrote was, "Most Asian assassins use knives and the woman was killed with a knife, therefore, the woman was killed by an Asian assassin." A good assumption, but I wouldn't bank my entire investigation on it. The next syllogism was more revealing to me. "Money is usually behind the hiring of an assassin. The woman was killed by an assassin, therefore the woman was killed because of a business deal gone sour."

I soon had more theories than pro basketball players have groupies. But the one that kept coming up had to do with Asian assassins. If my hunch was correct, the police weren't going to solve this murder in the foreseeable future, if at all.

If I concentrated on why our Asian Queen was murdered, while the police focused their efforts on who, with any luck, I could have something for Bill before they finished sifting through the forensic evidence.

I was engrossed in my battle plan when Bill poked his red-haired head into my office and informed me that I had a lunch meeting with Detective Rodney Bilbo in San Pedro.

If the police leads were as bad as the directions to my luncheon rendezvous, they were in deep trouble. I ended up sitting in heavy traffic, attempting to turn left on the corner of twenty-second and Gaffey. Just as I was about to give up, there was an opening.

This might be SOP (standard operating procedure) for the locals, but it's PYP (pee your pants) for those of us less accustomed to defying longevity odds just to go to lunch.

I continued down Twenty-second Street in search of the restaurant descriptively called The 22nd Street Landing. I guided the car into the parking lot that proudly announced I was entering San Pedro's favorite seafood restaurant. The restaurant was aptly named. Although the entrance faced the street, the structure itself was right on the landing to the San Pedro Yacht Basin where all sizes and shapes of pleasure craft rolled lazily at their moorings. It was a setting right out of the movies, directly responsible for a surge in immigration from the Midwest. The picture was made complete by the strategically placed palm trees next to the building, swaying in cadence with the rolling boats on the water.

As I was climbing up varnished wooden steps, I hoped that I would remember what Detective Bilbo looked like in the daylight. The one thing that I was quite sure of was, he wouldn't be in dress blues.

I need not have worried. You can take the cop out of

the uniform, but you can still spot him a mile away. Some day, somebody's going to have to clue these guys in that mustaches don't necessarily have to be part of the costume. There he was, the only person in the place with a bushy mustache and a bulge on the left hip, wearing a sport coat and wrinkled pants, and he was talking to a waitress. If there was ever a caricature of a cop, it was that very moment.

When I was first assigned to the police beat, the old man I replaced told me that if cops would spend as much time chasing the bad guys as they do chasing women, we could wipe out crime overnight. I was going to have to do some research on women cops to see if they worked that way too.

As soon as he saw me, he broke off the conversation. He must have already gotten her phone number. He motioned me to a prearranged table.

"So," he said, "you enjoying Southern California?"

"Yeah, sure," I replied, "I always look for a good old fashioned homicide to cover so I don't get homesick."

He managed a forced smile at my stab at humor. "Bill mentioned that you're going to help him out with the murder story. He also told me that you are one of Chicago's hottest reporters and asked me to treat you like the local guys."

I wondered if he let all the "local guys" buy him lunch the day after a murder was committed. But, wanting to start off on a positive note, I held my tongue.

Right on cue, our perky waitress appeared at the table. Bilbo ordered sea bass and iced tea. I ordered Idaho trout and a beer.

As soon as we were alone again, it was my turn to get

right to the point. "I appreciate your candor and the help. I want to assure you going in, that anything you tell me that you want off the record will be kept just that." If I've learned anything in all my years of digging, it's to respect sources, official and otherwise. In Los Angeles or in Chicago, you're only as good as your information, so your word has to be taken at face value.

He seemed to accept my statement and confirmed my suspicions. "Frankly, I don't think we're going to get much from the crime scene. It has all the marks of a professional hit. By tomorrow the lab will know the size and weight of the assailant, but little else. Just from what I saw, I would guess it was an Asian ... but you can't print that. Besides, if you did, without any hard evidence, it wouldn't be politically correct and you'd be accused of being a racist." This time the smile was real.

"Don't worry about me," I reassured him. "I wouldn't want to have half of Bill's subscribers cancel their subscriptions."

He broke off a piece of sourdough bread, offering me the basket. "The way the hill is going, it's going to be at least half Asian, heading toward two-thirds."

"That much?" I asked, buttering the end piece.

"It's getting there. It's not that much in the Estates, but when you get over to RPV, it's a lot heavier."

"RPV?"

"Forgot you're not from around here. That's short for Rancho Palos Verdes. They don't have their own department even though they're more heavily populated than we are. So they contact police services from the Sheriff. The ethnic make-up of the Peninsula has been getting more Asian every year, which is the reason people from Relondo and Torrance refer to it as the 'yellow hill.' Torrance shouldn't talk though, because UCLA has estimated that Asians will be 60% of that city's population within the next decade."

"Bill told me about the yellow hill references last night, and I wondered if this population change has brought an increase in hate crimes along with it?"

"No," said Bilbo. "It's been too gradual. Old timers grumble and people get pissed off because they can't get a tee time on the Los Verdes golf course, but there's no denying that the Asian influence has kept property values high. Companies like Toyota and Nissan, who have their American main offices in Torrance, have purchased housing on the Peninsula for their Senior Managers." He stopped talking as two customers passed by our table, then resumed when they were out of earshot. "The only problem occurs at the high school."

"How's that?"

"Asian kids take their studies a lot more serious than Anglo kids. Instead of playing ball after school, they do their socializing at the local library. The Anglos refer to the PV library as the Asian Community Center." He laughed at his own joke. "Also, with few exceptions, the Asian population doesn't assimilate into the community, but tends to socialize with their own kind. You find very few organizations on the hill that have an Asian membership even remotely consistent with their numbers. This has caused a certain amount of grumbling, but no outright hostility."

"So, what you're saying is, that you don't think the murder last night was a hate crime?"

"You know as well as I do that we don't discount

anything," said Bilbo. "But, on a scale of one to ten, I'd place it at a two."

I looked to make sure that no one had been seated near us before I asked, "Do I dare mention it?" Another quick glance around the room. "What do you make of the ears?"

He also scanned the room to verify that we were still in relative isolation. "As you can guess, that's something we definitely don't want to see in print. It's the one detail we have that will separate the kooks from the real thing if someone calls up to take responsibility."

The more we talked, the more I liked the guy. He didn't have that "I-know-everything" attitude that's so prevalent among so many of Chicago's senior detectives.

I assured him that I wouldn't even think about printing that information, though it would make a great headline.

He leaned forward and lowered his voice a few decibels. "I don't really know what to make of it. Right now, I'm inclined to think that it's proof of the killing so the person who made the hit can get paid. If that's the case, someone may want to view the body to be sure, so we'll be paying a lot of attention to those who pay the funeral home a visit. It also could be a trophy, which will be great evidence if we can catch the person who did this crime."

I couldn't resist. "I noticed you said 'if,' not 'when.'"

He leaned back in the chair again. "You know as well as I do, if this is a contract hit, the chance of finding the hit man is remote. We may eventually get the person who contracted for the hit, but not the hit man. Of course, to be politically correct, I should say hit person." This statement wasn't without humor, though there was a hint of sarcasm. That wasn't unexpected. In spite of the spin that the local public servants have put on the proliferation of women in the police departments, men aren't all that enthralled with the idea of having a one-hundred-and-fifteen-pound female as their primary backup.

I agreed with his premise, but added, "There is the possibility that the killer could be a female."

"True," he said. "And we might never know. From the indentations I saw, the killer was physically small. They could be female, Asian, or both."

We halted our conversation when the waitress came with our lunch.

Once she had retreated to the kitchen, I pulled out my notebook and bluntly asked him, "Can you give me any details about the victim such as name, maiden name, how long married, where she comes from, all those little details to track down? I'd like to find out the 'what' and 'who' about who this person really was?"

Ignoring my poised pen, he pulled a paper out of his sport coat and handed it to me. "This will give you everything. The husband's been very cooperative. They've only been married a little over three years, and he didn't know much about her life before that time. This is the press release the department has prepared about her."

I glanced at the paper. Asian female, age thirty-nine. name, Susan McCloskey, maiden name, Susan Wong. Married to Captain Tom McCloskey, age forty-five. occupation, Captain, Orient Airlines. Said female owned and operated U.S. Tours, a Hong Kong corporation specializing in tours of the United States for Far Eastern customers. That was it.

This lack of details only whetted my appetite for more information. I found myself eating faster so I could get out of this place. I had to talk to the husband. There was a lot more to Mrs. Susan Wong McCloskey that needed to be uncovered. Was it a coincidence that an Asian woman operating a travel service for Asian customers was murdered by an Asian hit man?

While I was searching for a way to break off lunch without offending Detective Bilbo, my dilemma was taken care of when he started to rise. "I have to be going. Good luck. If you come across anything important, I know you'll bring it to our attention."

The detective left. The check came and I paid, making sure I had a receipt. After stopping to take in the view one more time before I left, I retrieved my car and hoped I could find my way to the victim's house.

I was in luck. I found it even though the front entrance was now void of the yellow police line. It looked different in the daylight. The McCloskey house was the only one on the street that had two stories. All the rest were one story with red tile roofs.

Luck was running with me today, for, not only did I find the house, the husband was in it. In fact, he was just coming out of the side door when I pulled up. I identified myself and told him that I needed to talk with him.

His reply was the standard, "I told the police everything I know. Please leave me alone."

I've never known a successful reporter who ever let it go at that. Placing my body in his path, I replied, "Look, I know it's hard for you, and I won't take up much of your time. I'm not trying to look for tonight's headlines or do the police's work for them. I'm trying to find some background information about your wife, and I think you'll agree it's better for all concerned to get the correct information from someone who knows rather than gossip from the neighbors."

He bought it and invited me into the house. I craned my neck to see as much of the place as I could to get some feeling for the people who lived there. The side door opened into the kitchen. To my left was a formal dining room, with a living room beyond. Both rooms were decorated in a Chinese motif. My host turned right into a family room. I could see French doors leading from the back of the room out to a covered patio and kidney shaped pool. The family room had a more California contemporary look. I noticed a desk with a computer and printer, and a leather couch and a small cocktail table sitting on what looked to be an old cow skin. The pictures on the walls were of various airplanes. A few featured a much younger version of the man before me in uniform next to a Navy fighter plane.

It was obvious whom this room belonged to.

He didn't offer me a seat, so we stood face to face in the middle of the room.

"Look," he said, "I don't know much about my wife's life before we met. She said she was born in Montana, and she'd spent some time working in Hong Kong to get in touch with her Chinese roots. With the contacts she made there, she got an idea to open a travel and tour business to the States and eventually wound up in Los Angeles. Other than a birth certificate I found just this morning while I was looking for the key to her office, that's all I can really tell you. She always talked in past tense about her family, so I respected that and didn't pursue it."

I couldn't wait for him to finish so I could ask to see the birth certificate. He retrieved it from the desk. I immediately copied the information to my notebook. I noticed that she was born in Great Falls, Montana. I then asked about her business.

"I don't know too much about it," he said, finally gesturing for me to take a seat on a nearby couch. "She had an office in an executive suite in Rolling Hills Estates across from the library. I've only been there a couple of times. In fact, that's where I was headed when you showed up." He abruptly changed the subject. "I can't understand who would want to kill her. Do you have any ideas?"

The man before me was relatively calm and didn't appear to be a grieving widower. That bothered me, and I decided to say so. "First, I have to say that you seem to be taking your wife's death pretty well."

The bluntness of his answer surprised me. "I met my wife thirty-four months ago. We've been married for thirty of those thirty-four. I'm an airline pilot and make frequent trips to the Far East. She has her own business. We probably saw more of one another when she was on one of my flights to Hong Kong or Beijing than we did at home. When we were together, it was more for romantic interludes. There are no kids in the picture, nor would there ever have been any."

He repeated himself. "She had a career and a business, and so do I. We both knew going in that ours wouldn't be an old fashioned, Mid-Western marriage. Did I love her? Yes. Was it based more on physical love than mental love? I'd have to answer yes to that, too. So now you know. I'd rather that not be in print, if you don't mind."

I assured him that it wasn't in my immediate plans. I didn't tell him immediate meant the next issue, but that's as far as it went. He accepted my answer.

"Could you tell me how you met your wife?"

DEATH ON THE HILL

"She was on one of my flights to the Far East. As you can see by her picture," he pointed to a framed picture of her on one of the end tables, "she was a very attractive woman. One that any red blooded male would turn around to look at. I went back to get a cup of coffee and to stretch my legs as she was coming out of the latrine. She told me that she always wanted to see the inside of a cockpit, and asked if I would show it to her. I told her that I couldn't while we were in flight, but I would give her a tour after we had landed and were parked at the gate. The cockpit tour ended up with a dinner date, which eventually ended in our getting married."

"Whose idea was it to get married?"

He thought for a moment. "I guess it was hers. Never thought of it much. I sort of went along for the ride. Have to say, I never regretted it. Before we got on the subject of how we met, you never said if you had any ideas about her death."

I told him the truth. "It has all the earmarks of a professional killing. From what I saw, and from what I understand from the police—don't quote me to them, please— the person who did it doesn't appear to be an amateur."

"Do you think the police will ever find the killer?" he asked, taking a cigarette from the pack on the desk. He offered me one.

I refused and moved to the other end of the couch, as far away from the smoke as I could get, and said, "If it's a pro, they only kill for money. For the police to find out who actually did the killing, they would have to find out who paid for it to be done. That could be the tricky part. If I were to give odds, I'd give no more than a ten percent chance the actual killer will ever be found. Maybe a thirty or forty percent chance the police will find out who could have wanted her dead. Tying the two things together, maybe a twenty percent chance anyone will be hauled before a court to answer for the death of your wife."

"Those aren't very good odds no matter how you look at it," he replied blowing smoke away from me.

"No," I said, "they aren't. The police have a pretty narrow window in which to work. They have a lot of outstanding crimes to investigate. So, after awhile, things have a habit of slipping to the back burner. On the other hand, I can devote as much time as I need to get to the truth. Assuming, of course, that you will help me by piecing together your wife's past and present to arrive at who would want to see her dead."

His body language told me before he answered that he bought into my logic. "You can count on me. Maybe we didn't have an All-American marriage, but in our own way, we loved one another and she didn't deserve to go out the way she did. I only have one request."

"What's that?"

"I want to approve the stories before you print them."

"No can do," I told him. "I will tell you this, though, I won't make anything up. And if we find out something embarrassing that doesn't have a direct bearing on who killed your wife and why, I won't print it for the sake of sensationalism."

"I'll buy that," he said, standing up and extending his hand.

We shook on it.

"Now," I said, "after you give me a good picture of your wife, let's get started by going to her office and seeing what we can find."

CHAPTER THREE

The office of USA Tours was exactly what I had expected. The room was no larger than ten by twelve feet with a large picture window overlooking the street.

The decor looked to be mostly Chinese antiques with a fantastic table instead of a traditional desk as the centerpiece. I couldn't resist caressing its polished mahogany top and the ancient dragons coiled around the legs of the magnificent piece. There was a mahogany framed rice paper room divider, hand painted with the same dragon as the carving on the table legs. It effectively hid an ugly gray steel filing cabinet. Twin mahogany chairs with embroidered silk seats completed the furniture.

From the moment I walked through the door, something bothered me about the place.

McCloskey spotted it immediately. "It's the first time in my life that I ever saw a desk without a piece of paper on it. It doesn't even have any drawers to hide them." The remark, plus the fact that he didn't have a clue where anything was, backed up his previous statement that he wasn't a frequent visitor to his wife's office.

"Why don't we start with the contents of the filing cabinet," I suggested.

Luckily it was unlocked because there were no keys in

sight. This was also a clue that we weren't going to find much revealing information in it either. The files did show that Susan Wong-McCloskey was well organized. The first drawer we examined was arranged by tour groups the company had brought into the country, one every quarter of the year. The second contained more groups for previous years. When we came to the third drawer, we hit pay dirt. The first folders we looked at were bank statements. I got the impression when we placed them on the table that this was the first time McCloskey knew what his wife's business was really all about. The very last folder in the drawer contained two sealed envelopes.

"Be careful opening those," I cautioned. "Better use a letter opener. We don't want to destroy what might be evidence."

Our mouths dropped when he spread the contents of a file on the table. Staring up at us was the familiar face of Ben Franklin on a bundle of one hundred-dollar bills.

"I didn't know the travel business paid in cash," I said.

"It doesn't," replied McCloskey, "but I know that Sue had to grease a few palms in Beijing to cut through the red tape for some of the Chinese Nationals that wanted to come to the States. That's particularly true with those from Hong Kong after the takeover."

"Goes to show you, you can't hold a good capitalist down," I quipped, smiling.

McCloskey, on the other hand, spoke seriously. "Believe me, when it comes to good old fashioned bribery and kickbacks, the communist state officials are in a class by themselves."

"Good at it, huh?"

"Masters of the art," he smiled slightly. "Do you think I

should turn this over to the police?"

"I think you have to cover yourself and tell the police about it. Beyond that, I don't think I'd run to the local IRS office and declare it as income. If it's payoff money, your wife took it out of her accounts and didn't take it as a business deduction. The last time I looked, there wasn't a line on the tax form for that purpose."

"Look," he said, picking up the money and nervously inching his way toward the door, "I have an errand to run, so I'll just take this and see the PV police department on the way to tell them what I found."

Experience told me what would happen next. The police would want to come to the office and do what we were just doing. I needed time to go over the contents of the office a little more thoroughly before they came. "I need a couple of hours before they barge in here and seal it off, so why don't you run your errands and then tell the police about it?"

He agreed and left with the money. Realistically, I doubted that Bilbo or anyone else would ever know about the money.

As soon as I heard the outer door close, I looked for a copy machine. I didn't have much luck. The only one I could find was in the lobby for all suite residents. I didn't think they would look kindly upon a stranger copying the entire contents of their deceased tenant's file cabinets. I did the next best thing, and phoned Bill from a pay phone outside the building. I didn't know much about office suites, but I thought they usually kept records of telephone calls. If so, I didn't want the police finding a call to Bill's office.

Bill suggested that he send a couple of people over to

take the contents back to the paper and copy the files. Since the paper was less than a mile away, he estimated that it would take less than an hour to copy the entire contents of the filing cabinet and return them before the PV police arrived.

While I waited for Bill's crew to arrive, I started sorting the files to see what we could eliminate. I made an executive decision to just take case files at random, which would eliminate much of the bulk. I stacked everything I wanted to have copied, and Bill's people picked them up and took off again. In the meantime, I sat in Susan Wong-McCloskey's chair and surveyed the room.

On my second trip around the room, a picture on the wall caught my eye. It was a photograph of the deceased taken in what appeared to be a ballroom. People don't hang pictures of themselves standing next to ordinary customers. Usually it's with dignitaries or celebrities. I took a closer look. I definitely had seen the person standing next to the deceased before, but couldn't place him.

It had to be someone I had seen on the tube or in the papers. I made a mental note to follow-up. Another thing I have learned over the years is that you can usually tell the kind of person you are dealing with by the company that person keeps. When I learned more about this photograph, I'd know more about Mrs. McCloskey.

There was another interesting thing about the room. Except for that photograph, there was nothing else on the walls. Usually, in a person's office you see things like college degrees, pictures of spouses and kids, but in this one, nothing. I would have at least expected a picture of McCloskey decked out in his airline togs. Women like men in uniform, even if they're Greyhound bus drivers. Mrs. McCloskey apparently was the exception.

I had leads to follow and was cutting it close already, so I backed out of the office and made it to my car just as I spotted Detective Rodney Bilbo and two black-and-whites entering the executive suite parking lot.

Back at my office I plopped into my chair, placed my feet up on my desk and dialed the *Great Falls*, (Montana) *Tribune*. After a negotiated joint byline arrangement, and a promise of cooperation, the paper's managing editor promised to do some fast checking on Susan Wong and her family.

No sooner had I hung up the receiver when Bill was hovering over my left shoulder. "You have a story yet?" he asked anxiously.

"I've got one in the oven," I assured him. "I think we'll have an angle the other papers haven't caught on yet. I can feel it." I brought him up to date and explained the arrangement with the Great Falls Tribune.

He was hopping around like a Baptist Preacher on Easter Sunday. "We can't let anyone know what we're working on until it's too late for anyone else to go to press. Do you think you'll have enough to break this in the next edition?"

"We'll have something," I said, in the quietest tone I could muster. "But, it's asking a bit much to have the murder solved by then."

During our conversation, I kept thinking of Detective Bilbo. I hadn't wanted to embarrass him. I needed his cooperation, but his department obviously had links to the established Los Angeles media, namely the *Daily Breeze* and the *Los Angeles Times*. I mentioned this concern with

Bill.

"We have to share whatever we find out with Bilbo before he reads it in the paper," Bill replied. "I have to live with this guy. Make him look like a dummy in front of his chief and I'm in big trouble."

We decided that we would tell Bilbo what we had the evening before print, trusting him to tell no one except his Chief until the next morning. It was a chance we had to take, although we all knew that regular beat reporters have sources for confidential information within the department, just as the police have their stoolies on the streets. By telling him, though, rather than giving him something in writing, we had a chance to make it to press before Bill's competitors.

Then, in an instant brainstorm, it was my turn to get excited. I jumped up, pumping my arms in the air. "Yes, yes, that's it! That's the same guy. His name was Johnny something, I don't remember exactly, but he was the guy who arranged for the money from China to be filtered through the Democratic National Committee to the Clinton reelection campaign. Our little Miss Wong is chummy enough with him to get their picture taken together, and naive enough to plaster it on her office walls."

An embarrassed look came over Bill's face. "I have a confession to make. When that was going on, I was involved in getting the paper going and didn't pay much attention to the election. In fact, I'm embarrassed to say that I didn't even vote. I'm afraid you're going to have to take me to school on the facts."

I did.

"You remember during the mid-term elections in Bill Clinton's first term of office, the Democrats lost Congress to the Republicans. It was the first time in forty years that Republicans controlled both the House and the Senate. Clinton's substantial ego was really bruised. He vowed that he would win big when he ran for a second term. No doubt he thought that if he did, his coattails would be long enough so that his party would once again control the legislature.

"As a consequence, about a year before the national election he started raising money for his reelection campaign. Remember the furor when he, in effect, rented out the Lincoln bedroom in the White House to large campaign donors? Also, remember during that same time Vice President Al Gore attended a function at the Buddhist temple right here in Los Angeles, which turned out to be a fundraiser, which is illegal since the Buddhists enjoy tax exempt status as a religion."

"Yeah, I remember that."

"Even though you didn't vote, you must remember that before the election, the Democratic National Committee ran an advertising campaign that attacked the Republican Party and Bob Dole, the Republican front runner for the Republicans, before the campaign actually began. That, in itself, wasn't illegal, but our laws forbid candidates from taking part in such a campaign. However, it was pretty well proven that, not only did Clinton take part in that strategy, he also participated in formulating the ads.

"Anyway, a vast sum of money was raised by the Democrats for the Clinton campaign by Asian interests, including a check from some high Communist Chinese military figure. The money went directly into the 'Clinton for President' treasury, which is illegal since Clinton applied for, and received, matching funds from American taxpayers, which forbids such a practice to be eligible for taxpayer funds. The front person for the Chinese was that guy in the picture."

"Wait," Bill said. "If she was involved in something like that, why get your picture taken and hang it for everyone to see?"

"You're right, which is why we have to find someone in the local Asian community to help us in this thing. The question is who? Neither you nor I have those contacts, and how in the hell are we going to cultivate them in time to do us any good?"

"I'm sure the Sheriff's Department has them. I'm not sure the Palos Verdes Police Department does. However, small departments like the Estates do have a detective or two from the LA County Sheriff's Department assigned to help them out. In fact, I think most of them already have contracts in place for just this type of emergency."

"Crime doesn't respect city limits," I replied.

"You got that right. Particularly in Los Angeles." He went over to a map of the Los Angeles/Orange County area hanging on the wall. "Just look at the beach cities. Go north on Pacific Coast Highway. From PV you go to Torrance, then Redondo Beach, then Hermosa Beach, then Manhattan Beach, then El Segundo, then Los Angeles, all within eighteen miles at the outside."

He traced the area along the water. "Going South, you go from Torrance to Lomita, to Harbor City, to Wilmington, to San Pedro, to Long Beach, to Seal Beach, and so on until you get to San Diego a hundred and twenty odd miles away. That's a lot of geography, and an equal amount of jurisdictions."

It might not be polite, but as Bill was talking, my mind

was concentrating on the problem. I wasn't naive enough to think that either the Sheriff or the PV police would give us preferential information. But I knew how to network.

I politely shooed Bill away. "You get on with your weddings and sorority parties for sixty-year-old cheerleaders and over-the-hill flight attendants, and let me work on finding some sources within the Asian community."

Although there's a three-hour time difference between the West Coast and DC, Washington Bureau Chiefs don't respect the clock. The problem was, I had left my address and telephone information on my desk computer, which was back in Chicago.

I called my editor in Chicago to get Stan's number.

The first thing he said after I asked for Stan's number was, "I thought you were taking a vacation?" The second thing was, "If you're working on anything we can use, remember who signs your paycheck."

I assured him that all I was doing was a favor for a friend and not to get his balls in an uproar. Typically, he told me he was too busy to run errands for me, and turned me over to the Washington desk, which I should have called in the first place.

I tried Stan's office first. No answer. Next, I dialed his home number where I woke up his wife to find out that he wasn't home yet. I left messages at both places, then tried his beeper, hoping he'd at least have it on the vibrator mode so it would give him a thrill and put him in a good mood to call me back. That worked. He called me from his car within fifteen minutes.

If there was anyone in Washington who had connections, it was our Washington Bureau Chief. Stan

Wasnewski had cut his journalistic teeth in the trenches of Chicago's ward politics.

When Dan Rostenkowski was elected to Congress and had gone to Washington, Stan followed. As Dan progressed, Stan was working himself up the ladder of the paper's Washington establishment. When Stan proved his loyalty covering Rostenkowski's fall from power after a scandal, he was named Chief of the Washington Bureau, assuming all the power and headaches that went with it.

What made Stan so effective was the way he could blend his Polish bullheadedness with a charm so well oiled that he literally oozed his way into the inner sanctums of the powerful House Committee Chairmen. Although he made sure the Senate was covered, he spent his time at the House of Representatives, knowing it was the newsworthy body. I knew that if anyone could network me into the Asian community in Los Angeles, it would be Stan.

I quickly dispensed with the formalities. I told him everything, emphasizing the photograph I had found on the wall of the travel agency, blowing its role completely out of proportion.

Stan took the bait. "I'll get back to you within the hour with some names. This could be hot stuff and just the spin I can use here. So far, we haven't been able to get much more than a 'business as usual' reaction from the public. But if we can tie a juicy murder to it, I'll be on every Sunday morning talk show in town, and we'll sell a ton of papers."

"Don't tell Bob Woodward to move over and make room for you yet," I cautioned. "This is still a long shot, and we don't have much to go on." Woodward was the *Washington Post* reporter who broke the Nixon Watergate scandal.

"Yeah," he replied. "But as we learned in the first grade, from little acorns mighty oaks grow."

"I'll wait right here for your call." I hung up before he started quoting Shakespeare.

Less than an hour later Stan called back with the names and telephone numbers of no less than four people for me to talk with. Armed with that information, I went out for something to eat and back to Bill's house. I knew that tomorrow was going to be one busy day.

CHAPTER FOUR

The people in Montana worked fast. I could hear the anxiety in the *Great Falls Tribune* editor's voice. "I got another copy of the birth certificate, and a little bonus along with it. I also have a death certificate dated four and a half years ago."

"You sure it's the same person?" I asked, bolting upright in my chair.

"Sure am. The only way I found out was the clerk that issued both still works for the county. When I talked to her about getting a birth certificate for Susan Wong born thirty nine years ago, she asked me if I also wanted the death certificate."

"Talk about luck," I replied, not even trying to disguise my excitement. "We just fell in it."

The thought struck me that we should carry the investigation a little further. I asked him to have the clerk make a list of the deaths of people of Asian descent for the past five years by name and age at death. Then she should cross-reference the list to requests for duplicate birth certificates.

I didn't know where all of this was going to lead, but "from tiny acorns mighty oaks grow." I cautioned him to keep this quiet for a while so we could break the story together, if there was one. I could tell from the editor's voice that he shared my enthusiasm. Achieving emotional orgasms on mere threads of exciting news is one thing that all reporters have in common. On a good day, one could go home a sexual cripple.

We hung up, agreeing to touch base when we had something to report.

I went on with my networking. I dialed the first number on the list that Stan had given me. Today was my lucky day. I reached a person rather than an answering machine and voice mail.

I noticed right off that the voice that answered didn't have an accent. I must have sounded hesitant after I identified myself and asked, "I'm looking for Sidney Lu. Stan Wasnewski suggested I call."

"This is Sidney. Or were you expecting Charlie Chan to answer the phone."

I didn't know if he was defensive or had a sense of humor. I answered in my best professional tone. "Did Stan tell you I would be calling?"

"He told me, and why. I've read about the case in the *Times*."

"Then he also told you that I'm looking for some ears into the community."

"Yeah, he told me that, too. But I don't feel comfortable talking at any length over the telephone. Let's set up a meeting. I'm free for lunch tomorrow."

"Sounds good to me. Here or there?"

"Neither," he replied. "Let's do it in Santa Monica. Say, Madam Wu's at eleven thirty. I'll let you buy me lunch."

"That's gracious of you," I said, reverting back to my

true character. I can carry a personality facade only so far.

Now, all I had to do was find out where Madam Wu's was and how to get there, and I would be in business. But first, I had three more people to call. I didn't see the necessity to act like I had a deep dark secret to protect.

Stan was enough of a pro that he would give me only solid contacts, and the more probes I had out there the better my chances of ferreting out something I could use. I also didn't think that I should worry much about the *Breeze* and *Times* finding out about the birth and death certificates until my first story came out.

I was sure that once our paper hit the street, it would grab the attention of a sharp editor in one of those publications. Then, they and the police would be concentrating in the same place. I couldn't help but smile when I thought of the scenario. It could resemble an old Mack Sennett comedy with everyone converging on their Asian sources at the same time. Chinatown informants would feel like quiz show contestants. The only problem was, that under this same scenario the *Times* would likely come out the clear winner. It was doubtful that the *Daily Breeze*, being a regional publication, would be in the ball game when the heat was turned on. They simply wouldn't have the resources.

Unfortunately, neither did I, so I had to rely on quickness. I began to wonder if I should sit on the birth certificate and death certificate lead a little longer. The only thing wrong with that was the husband. He had blabbed it to me. There was nothing to keep him from doing the same thing to the competition or the police. The same was true for the travel office. Indeed, the police might have already identified the person in the picture and started to make inquiries.

When I called the next name on Stan's list, I wasn't so lucky. I got my old nemesis—voice mail.

I left my message, which was never returned, and dialed numbers three and four, ending up with two more appointments for the next day—one at three in the afternoon at an office downtown in the Biltmore Tower and another actually in a Chinatown restaurant for dinner.

I ignored them as long as I could, but staring at me was a pile of papers that contained all the copied material from the travel agency office. I started to sift through the contents, beginning with the bankbook. Not surprisingly, it was from the Bank of Hong Kong.

I started copying down items that caught my eye, making a list of dates and amounts of deposits. There were a couple of large disbursements made out to cash that needed to be reconciled with the group folders. Other than that, all it contained were entries for the suite rental, and a post office box. I also jotted down the name of a health club that appeared every month.

Another folder that caught my eye was marked "loan." There, I found loan papers made out to Susan Wong for an unsecured loan of $150,000. I looked back in the checkbook copies to see if she was making payments on the loan. I didn't find anything. I wrote the name of the loan officer in my notebook and kept plodding along.

It wasn't yet noon, so I thought I would take the rest of the day off with pay and actually do one of the things that I had come to California for. I was going to have lunch near the beach and look at all the pretty blonde California girls.

I left the office without telling Bill where I was going, and I didn't feel the least bit guilty.

I jumped in the Enterprise rental car that Bill had graciously arranged to have delivered to the office and headed toward Rivera Village. I'd been told that they serve great burgers at a place called the Brewery on Catalina Avenue where you can sit outside and do what California bachelors do best—watch women.

The beach cities along Santa Monica Bay have an abundance of single people who work nights so they can spend their time either sunning on the beach, walking or jogging along the beach, or sitting in places like the Brewery impressing each other with their coolness.

Since I don't jog, and I was hungry and still smarting from a sunburn, I chose the later. It took me one beer and the time it takes to order a hamburger to find out my waitress's name was Lucinda. On the second beer, I found out she was of Mexican ancestry. It took the third beer to find out she lived about three blocks away and was free for dinner that night.

Since my dinner date wasn't until 7:00 PM, and I didn't feel like going back to work, I had plenty of time to kill. So, I did what any forty-year-old bachelor full of micro brew and a hot date that evening would do. I went home to take a nap.

I was asleep before my head made contact with the pillow.

I had left a note for Bill telling him to wake me by five-thirty. I didn't say anything about having a date. He'd think it was business and be sure that I was up. Lucky thing I did, because the next thing I remember was Bill shaking me. I probably would have slept through the night.

I was parked in front of Lucinda's apartment before 6:30, trying to decide if I should go to the door early.

I sat in the car debating the situation. If I went up early, it would look like I was overly anxious. On the other hand, it wouldn't hurt to signal her my interest. Who was I kidding? She knew I was interested, or I wouldn't have come on to her at the restaurant.

I got out of the car and took a walk to kill some time. I knocked on her door at six fifty. She was ready. I took that as a positive sign.

"You know this area better than I do," I said. "Where should we go?" I was still standing in the middle of her living room since she hadn't invited me to sit down.

"What do you feel like eating?" she asked.

"How about seafood?"

"Great," she replied. "That sounds good to me."

Well, so far so good. We made it to the type of food we were going to have. Now all we had to do was decide on a place to have it.

She cleared that up pretty quickly. "There's a place on the Peninsula that's supposed to be good. It's called the Admiral Risty. Why don't we go there?"

"Lead the way," I said, as I opened the apartment door and led her down the steps to where I was parked.

"You're lucky you found a place to park so close," she told me as I guided her to the car. "Usually, this time of the night all the places are taken by people coming home from work."

I couldn't resist. "This has been my lucky day, starting with choosing to eat at the Brewery, and picking your table."

She managed a giggle.

DEATH ON THE HILL

I was parked in the wrong direction so I had to make a U-turn at the next light.   It gave me time to think of something to say. I wasn't having much luck. There I was, a hot shot bachelor reporter and nothing to say, so I did what all good reporters do, I asked her about herself, and she accommodated me.

I now knew that Lucinda came from a family of three girls, and she attended the University of Southern California where she majored in marketing. After school, a marketing firm that had a client wanting to break into the Hispanic market had hired her. Being Hispanic, she had been hired to provide the bridge between the Anglo firm and the Hispanic culture they had wanted to target.

It hadn't worked out, and she had been let go. She'd had trouble landing another job and had started waitressing to pay the rent.

That had been over a year ago. In the meantime, she'd been offered to get back into the business world.

It didn't make any sense to me, but what do I know? Journalism didn't pay worth a damn either, but I'd be darned if I'd leave it to wait tables. I held my tongue and soon we were speeding along Palos Verdes Drive West toward the restaurant.

The Admiral Risty was in a shopping center directly across from the ocean. If one ignored the cars zooming by on PV Drive, the view was spectacular, particularly at sunset, which it happened to be when we arrived. If I could have found a way to take credit for the timing I would have.

As we were being led to a table, a familiar face came into view. Waving at me from one of the tables was the only person beside the murdered woman's husband and my friend Bill, whom I knew in Los Angeles. Detective Rodney Bilbo and a slightly overweight, but cute, blonde, which I assumed to be his wife. Even cops wouldn't be brazen enough to bring a girlfriend to a popular eating establishment in the same town where they worked.

Bilbo was the last person I wanted to talk to, so I nodded hello, muttered a "nice to see you," and moved on.

As we moved into the next room, engrossed in serious conversation with a very attractive Asian woman sat none other than Captain Tom McCloskey, widower all of three days.

The mourning period in Southern California must be a lot shorter than where I come from. In fact, the grieving widower hadn't had time yet to claim the body from the county morgue.

He didn't see me, and I didn't make myself conspicuous. Fortunately, Lucinda and I were seated where I was hidden by two other tables. I could watch him, but he couldn't see me—a perfect situation.

I wondered if the presence of Bilbo in the next room had anything to do with the presence of McCloskey. Hell, I was working whether I liked it or not, and resented it. I didn't want anything to disrupt my evening with the enchanting Lucinda.

As the evening progressed, I glanced at McCloskey less and less. Not only was my companion beautiful, she was intelligent and had a wonderful sense of humor. Unlike the other women I had come in contact with since I had been here, she wasn't into herself. She actually had other interests, one being the obvious pride she felt about her Hispanic heritage.

Things were going well between Lucinda and me. So

well that I didn't want the evening to end. But the United States isn't Europe. The last morsel of food was no sooner off my plate when the waiter came to take it away. I have always felt that it is in bad taste to start clearing the table while someone at the table was still eating, so I told the waiter to leave it. I asked Lucinda why they did this.

She laughed. "The management tells them to. The quicker you get the table cleared, the quicker they leave and give the table to someone else."

"Let's frustrate them tonight and linger a while over coffee and desert."

"I'll take decaf coffee, but pass on the desert."

"You're good for me. You have this uncanny ability to suppress my decadent tendencies."

This got a wicked laugh out of her. "We haven't come far enough in our relationship for me to keep you from overdosing on fat and cholesterol."

I couldn't let that opening pass. "At least you're holding out hope for me that we may have a relationship brewing here. That's encouraging."

Lucinda was quick on the uptake. "I guess a person can assume when they get picked up and taken out to dinner, there was something that sparked it. There's always a possibility that initial infatuation will turn into a relationship, otherwise why start?"

Sometimes I say stupid things. This was one of those times. "There's always a possibility of someone just wanting a free meal."

"I can afford to buy my own meals, thank you," she quickly replied, a defiant look on her face.

I made an effort to repair the damage and said in the sincerest voice I could come up with, "I didn't mean to imply that I was referring to you. I was merely pointing out another possibility, so please don't read anything different into it. After all, I am a reporter, so a certain amount of skepticism is natural for me."

She furrowed her brow and gave me an over-the-eyeglasses look, except she didn't wear glasses. "Should I know who you are?"

"No. I'm no one you would know about. Just a working reporter." At least I had enough sense not to tell her I worked for a Chicago paper. That could really foul up the evening by placing her in the one-night-stand category.

"What paper?"

I didn't lie. "Right now it's the *Peninsula Digest*. A friend of mine owns it. You probably never heard of it."

"Oh yes I have," she replied. "When I worked for a marketing company in Malaga Cove Plaza, we used to subscribe to the paper. It's mostly local news, so I didn't read it. I preferred the *Times*."

"Yeah," I said, mimicking Bill. "Local weddings, Junior League, and overage sorority parties are its forte', with an occasional murder thrown in for good measure."

"You must be talking about that Chinese woman that got killed up here the other day. Are you covering that?"

Everyone likes to feel important and impress their date, and I'm no exception, so I said, "Sure am. In fact, if you sneak a peek, two tables over you'll see the husband of the victim with another woman."

After looking back over her shoulder, she said, "He's not wasting any time, is he?"

"Don't draw any conclusions by the company he's keeping. Note that it's an Asian woman about the same age as his former wife. No laughing and giggling like two school kids. And, hey. A person has to eat."

"Still," she replied, "if you really love someone, you don't feel like going out with another person, even for business purposes, a couple of days after your wife is murdered."

"They had only known each other for a little more than three years before she was killed."

"Well," said Lucinda, "I know I certainly wouldn't feel like it."

"Oh, well, nothing we can do about it either way. But it would be interesting to find out where they go after they leave here."

She quickly picked up on my comment. "Why don't we follow them when they leave? They're even taking longer to finish eating than we are. They were already eating when you pointed them out to me."

I don't normally like to involve amateurs in my investigations, but one doesn't squander an opportunity that drops into your lap either. Besides, she was very observant, so I agreed.

We followed McCloskey and the woman at a discreet distance out of the restaurant. Once out the door we went directly to the rental car as the other two stopped to talk by a white Jaguar parked closer to the restaurant. I noticed that he didn't even kiss her on the cheek as he opened the door to help her into the vehicle. She drove off alone.

The Jaguar turned right out of the parking lot, back along the coast the way we had come from Redondo Beach.

My underpowered Toyota was no match for the Jag's power plant as she sped around the winding road up the hill. I lost her several times, but she always managed to come back into view when the street curved back into my line of sight.

After I thought I had lost her for good, Lucinda cried out excitedly, "There she is. Going up that driveway over there." She pointed toward a large home just as the iron gates were closing.

"Get the number as we pass," I told her. "I don't want to slow down just in case someone is watching." Tomorrow I would check the tax records to see who owned the property.

I was thinking of this when Lucinda said, "What do we do now?"

"Consider this just a brief intermission in a delightful evening and continue on with what we were doing, which was ...?"

She completed the sentence for me, "Taking me home so I can get up in the morning because I have the early shift."

That put a hold on what I had in mind, but I didn't consider it a permanent setback. Just a bump in the road between first date and first time.

I turned the car around and headed back down the hill, my mind going back and forth between my attractive companion and the equally attractive Asian woman who had just disappeared behind a wrought iron gate.

My attention was suddenly diverted when, as I was approaching a sharp curve at the bottom of the hill, headlights appeared behind me from out of nowhere. The Toyota lurched forward when the bumper of the pursuing vehicle made contact. Lucinda screamed as I tried to keep the Toyota under control as the car behind us accelerated. I had to make a split second decision whether to try and manipulate the curve and probably overturn, or continue ahead through the white picket fence that was looming ahead.

I chose the picket fence. I didn't think whoever was pushing us against our will would follow.

Splintered wood flew in all directions as the Toyota tore through the fence into the yard. Luckily for us, it was a deep yard. By the time I managed to stop the car, about three feet from the house, the other car had disappeared.

It was only a matter of seconds before lights went on in the house. I geared myself for an angry verbal barrage when a man clad in blue shorty pajamas came tearing out of the house. "Are you all right?"

"We're fine," I replied, as we got out of the car. "We had our seatbelts on."

"I always knew this was going to happen someday." The homeowner was surprisingly calm for someone who just had a car tear through his yard.

I went to the rear of the car to check for dents. The bumper wasn't even dented, nor was the trunk. Great, I thought, no one's going to believe that I was pushed. I could hear Lucinda telling the homeowner the story. My day was complete when I heard the siren approaching from a distance.

The friendly face of Officer Susan Constable got out of her patrol car.

The first thing out of my mouth was, "You left your lights on, Officer." She looked at me and smiled. "Thank you for that bit of information, but who is the driver of this vehicle?"

"I am," I replied giving her my best smile.

"Is anyone hurt?" she asked.

"No one," I replied. "We were in seat belts."

Lucinda was soon at my side. "Someone tried to run us off the road."

The homeowner chimed in behind her. "It looks to me that they succeeded. Look at my lawn."

By this time the neighborhood was totally alerted and gathering on their neighbor's lawn. This made me feel like a marked man.

Witty Lucinda looked at me and started to laugh. "It's a good thing you're not cheating on your wife."

Arriving back at her apartment house, I had to double park, and I was just starting to elevate my arm when she remarked, "I have to say one thing for you, you sure know how to make a date exciting."

My arm made it around her shoulders. "The next time will be better, I promise. We'll do something a little safer, like skydiving."

Her goodnight kiss made it clear that there would be a next time.

CHAPTER FIVE

I awakened early after spending most of the night fantasizing about what I would do the next time I saw Lucinda. Unfortunately, however, I was facing a pretty full day and needed to put her out of my mind.

I thought I had better start my day with Detective Bilbo to get my being run off the road out of the way first. Next, I had to face the music with the rental car agency and swap cars. Following that, in order, would be: lunch with Sidney Lu at Madam Wu's in Santa Monica—I wondered if there was a relationship there; a meeting at the Biltmore Towers at three with Carleton Yang; and dinner at the Mandarin Palace with Sun Fu Yee.

In between those events, I had to bang out a story for the paper. It had to go to press that night for the morning edition, which meant that I had to strategize with Bill and also talk to Captain McCloskey. I was sure the news that his wife wasn't really Susan Wong would come as a surprise to him, and if I wanted to keep him as an information source he shouldn't find out about it in the morning.

Bill was in the kitchen when I made my appearance downstairs. He had already seen the rental car. "What in the hell did you run into last night? You get bombed and hit something?"

"Nothing that simple." I filled him in on the details of my evening.

"We've got to bring Bilbo up to date. Could you find the house where you followed the woman? The car that came after you must have come from there."

"It was dark and on a road that was as crooked as a politician," I commented. "I can only say for sure that it had a wall around it with an Iron Gate. I thought I had the address written down, but I can't find it."

"You've just described at least a half dozen houses on that stretch of road. You have to do better than that."

"Sorry," I said. "That's the best I can do."

"Damn, if you could spot it, it might be the break we're looking for."

I followed him outside and said, "Look. The woman in the car was Asian, so it's simple. I get a list of the Asians who live in that vicinity and we can narrow it down from there."

"We might be able to eliminate one or two entertainers, but that's all. Maybe Bilbo will have some ideas when you talk to him, and let's not forget to give the car back to the rental company. I know they're going to be thrilled."

"I hope you took out the insurance."

"Knowing you'd be the driver," he said, "you better believe I did. There's orange juice in the fridge if you want some. And water, of course."

I declined. Instead, I went over my schedule with him. He suggested that as soon as we write the story, we call Bilbo and have him meet us after my dinner to go over it. Bilbo wouldn't be too happy with the scheduling, because he'd have to call his Chief at home so he wouldn't be surprised when reading the paper in the morning.

Bill suggested that when I talked to Bilbo later this morning, I tell him about what was to come, without revealing the exact story, so he could alert his Chief and save some embarrassment for all concerned.

I left Bill and called Bilbo. He was in. He let me tell him the whole story before informing me he had already gotten the details from Officer Constable.

"Do you think you could point the house out to me?" he asked.

I gave him the same answer I had given Bill, and he replied similarly.

"So where do we go from here?" I inquired.

"For starters, you should stop following women in cars in the middle of the night. Especially people who employ bodyguards."

"You think that's it? The people that ran me off the road were bodyguards that wanted to scare me?"

"Could be."

"I don't buy it. It's just too much of a coincidence that the woman was having dinner with a guy three days after his wife was murdered."

"Stranger things have happened," said Bilbo. "If you remember, I was there too. But you didn't see *me* following the woman back to her house, now, did you?"

I was beginning to feel like a school kid who just got caught peeking into the girl's locker room. I decided to switch the subject a bit. "There's something else I need to talk to you about. I have to get some breakfast and wondered if you'd like to meet me for a cup of coffee? It's regarding the story I'm writing for tomorrow's paper. I don't want you to be surprised by it."

That got his attention. "Let's meet at a little sidewalk cafe right around the corner from the Police Department."

"I'll be there in fifteen minutes."

I jumped in my dented Toyota and was there in twenty minutes.

This had to be the most interesting sidewalk cafe I had ever been to. It wasn't because the tables were actually on the sidewalk that made it unique, but because the sidewalk was on a steep grade. The tables and chairs actually had wooden blocks under them to compensate. But, if you moved a couple of inches in either direction you could find yourself eating with a list, starboard or port, depending on your place at the table.

Once again, Detective Bilbo had beaten me, and was already nursing a cup of coffee. "So how's Evel Knievel today?" he greeted.

"Is that the thanks I get for helping you do your job?"

"What do you want the department do? Put you on the payroll?" He answered his own question. "No thanks. Our insurance policy excludes daredevils."

"Har har har. I literally sacrifice my life for you guys in blue and all I get is abuse. You see if I ever do that again."

"Do I have your word on that?"

"Never," I replied. "Haven't you heard that a reporter will do anything for a story?"

A waitress appeared.

Before Bilbo answered, I ordered leaded coffee and a bagel with good old fat-and-cholesterol-laden cream cheese. After all the healthy stuff I had been eating, it was going to be a pleasure to clog a few arteries and experience some taste for a change.

After she left, I followed her with the practiced eyes of

a man who has a genuine appreciation for firm, young female rear ends. When I refocused my eyes on Bilbo, I said, "You might be interested to know that this is the first time in the history of the Palos Verdes Estates Police Department that anyone has ever complained they were forced off the road on purpose."

Bilbo responded with, "You said you wanted to talk to me about what you're going to publish tomorrow."

"Our agreement was that I would keep you informed of what I was coming up with. Well, my problem now is that I have what I think is going to be my lead for the story, subject to one more verification." I lied a little here. "Unfortunately, I won't have that until after dinner tonight. I can say this, though. If all checks out, it will turn out to be something pretty startling." *I should have majored in drama instead of journalism. I could've made a lot more money.* "I really can't tell you anymore than that until tonight. Just wanted to give you a 'heads up' so I can contact you if I get verification. And so you can do the same with your Chief."

I could tell by the look on his face that he wasn't very happy with what he was hearing. "So you want me to call my chief, tell him that the *Peninsula Digest* will be coming out with a story on the case that we don't know about yet, but will make us look like a bunch of blundering idiots? Now it's my turn, my friend. How do you know that we haven't already discovered the same thing, and found it to be false?"

"Easy," I said. "Because I won't print it unless I have it verified, so I know it's right. It won't make any difference if you have it or not. All I care about is that the facts are right."

He seemed a little miffed. I could tell by the way he moved around in his chair. "You're telling me that as long as it's sensational and sells papers you don't care if it might hamper the investigation?"

He was sharp all right, but I wasn't going to fall into his trap.

Making sure that my body language matched my words, I calmly replied in as firm a voice as I could muster, without raising the volume. "I'm going to write it up and tell you about the contents after dinner tonight. If you think it'll hamper your investigation in any way, show me how, and we'll reconsider printing it."

The detective knew I wasn't bluffing. "I guess I'll hear from you tonight," he said, as he drained his cup and left. He was content to have the last word, leaving me to pay the check.

Breakfast completed, and after one more look at my waitress's firm little tush, I proceeded to my next appointment.

At the car rental company, the manager was unhappy after he surveyed the hood and grill. It was liberally sprinkled with dents, scrapes, and white paint. He reluctantly replaced the battered Toyota with another. I noticed that he didn't give me one of his newer models.

By this time, it was after nine-thirty and I still had to go to the paper, talk Bill into a laptop computer to write my story in the car between appointments, and get directions to Madam Wu's Chinese restaurant.

Getting the computer was easy. Finding my way to Madam Wu's in Santa Monica wasn't. I'd made the fatal mistake that all visitors to Los Angeles make. I'd assumed that between morning rush hour and lunch I could just breeze up the freeway. I got on the San Diego Freeway northbound only to come to a complete stop before I got as far as the airport. It was stop-and-go traffic all the way.

My directions were to go west on Wilshire. It seemed like I was going to end up at the beach before I spotted the restaurant on my right. Looking at my watch, I congratulated myself on being only fifteen minutes late.

Pulling into the parking lot, I wondered if the place was open, or if there was more than one Madam Wu's. The place was almost deserted.

When I cautiously pulled on the door to the restaurant, it opened. I went past massive fish tanks lining the outer lobby and was greeted by an ancient, but still beautiful, Chinese woman. I asked for Sidney Lu and was led through two rooms whose walls were covered with autographed photographs of old movie stars. I felt like I had just stepped back forty or fifty years in time. She deposited me at a small private room in the rear of the building.

The person who stood to meet me had to be Harvard Business School, circa 2000. My car was older than him. Talk about oxymorons. I was meeting with a child in an establishment one step removed from silent pictures. I felt like saying, "Oy vei," and I'm not even Jewish. He must have seen the look on my face.

"The last time we talked, I asked you if you expected Charlie Chan. Now I know that's the case."

"Sorry," I said lamely. "I'll admit that you aren't what I expected. Usually people I meet through Stan aren't as presentable." I thought I made a good recovery, but he wasn't fooled.

"Don't worry. I just have a young face."

"It's not just that. It has more to do with circumstances."

"Madam Wu is an institution in Los Angeles. My father was active in Los Angeles politics when the Oriental community was supposed to be seen and not heard, or at least not heard from. He wielded great power in backroom meetings. I have always admired and respected him. He accomplished a lot for the Chinese people in California. He was very good at both counting and delivering votes."

"And votes is what politicians understand."

"And votes is what politicians understand," he mimicked.

I tightened my lips as a waiter appeared at the door.

"You don't have to stop speaking in front of the waiter.

Madam Wu has assigned us a waiter who does not understand English. Which is why I will have to order for you, if you don't mind."

"I guess if I mind, I don't eat."

"You could point to the items on the menu, and have a reasonable chance that you will get what you want."

"You go ahead and order," I replied. "I don't believe there's anything on the menu that I won't eat."

Sidney Wu didn't bother to look at the menu and ordered in Chinese, then turned back to me. "Stan only told me that you were working on the Palos Verdes murder of a Chinese woman. He asked that I give you whatever assistance I could."

I spent the next fifteen minutes, without interruption, telling him everything I knew about the case, including why I was working on it.

When I had finished, he said, "And you want me to find out what the community knows?"

"You know that a reporter works on sources. I have zip in this town. Someone knows who and why that woman was killed. Not only that, someone knows who she really was, because we know that she wasn't the Susan Wong born in Great Falls, Montana."

Cocking his head to one side, a serious expression crossed his face. "My initial reaction is, that it will be difficult and possibly dangerous. The Chinese, the Koreans and the Japanese, all have the equivalent of the Mafia in this country. And just like the Mafia, they have ties to the homelands. They are much more ruthless and efficient than the Mafia, for they operate in a society closed to occidentals. They have never been infiltrated by the FBI, and generate no publicity."

"That's why I need someone like you to help me. Another thing. I've told you everything about me and the case, but I know nothing about you."

His expression didn't change. "I am a third generation American, born and raised in Los Angeles. I graduated from Stanford in political science. After graduation, I used my father's many connections to work for a local councilman whose constituency encompassed Chinatown. When the councilman didn't get reelected, our many friends at city hall saw to it that I received a good position. I'm currently assigned to community relations as liaison between the city and the Chinese community."

I had mixed feelings. He would certainly be in the know among the establishment, but I wasn't sure about his street knowledge. Another concern of mine was that Los Angeles, like most large cities in America, was primarily Democratic. I wasn't sure if he would do me any good because of the murder victim's tie to a prominent Asian

Democratic fundraiser.

What the hell! I decided to get what I'd come for. "What I'd like for you to do, is to find out if there are any ties between these people and to make some discreet inquiries about the murdered woman.

"I promise you," he said, "I'll see what I can find out."

I left hoping for the best, but not expecting much.

It was only about 12:45 when I left Madam Wu's. My next appointment wasn't until three, so I had some time to work on my story. I had it pretty well formulated in my mind, but I do my best work when my fingers are on the keyboard.

I got back in my Toyota and headed east toward downtown Los Angeles. I was looking forward to the trip. I'd never been there before. In fact, I hadn't even known that Los Angeles had a downtown.

As I was driving past UCLA in Westwood, and about to enter Beverly Hills, I thought of Herb Caen, the now deceased columnist for the *San Francisco Chronicle*, and no admirer of the City of Angels. He had described Los Angeles as "seventeen suburbs looking for a city." *Well, Herb, old buddy, I'm about to find that elusive city.*

Actually, before proving Herb wrong, I came upon a restaurant with an interesting name—The Hamburger Hamlet—and I decided to have a cup of coffee there and work on the story.

I made the birth certificate my lead. Since both the *Breeze* and the *Times* had two full days of reporting the story and we hadn't yet said a word about it, it took me awhile to get my thoughts together. I settled on "Mystery Woman Murdered in Palos Verdes Home" as my headline. After going through the details of the death, I followed with:

> The *Digest* has learned that
> the deceased had a falsified birth
> certificate. The certificate was
> the property of a woman born in
> Great Falls, Montana, who died
> 4 1/2 years ago.
>
> The *Great Falls Tribune*, working
> with the *Digest*, confirmed that Susan
> Wong's birth certificate was actually
> that of a woman from Great Falls.
> Further checking by the *Tribune*
> turned up a death certificate in the
> Great Falls area for that same person.
> The real Susan Wong's family was
> not available to comment regarding
> this bizarre mystery.

I thought that should grab attention and sell more than a few papers off the newsstands for Bill. I continued with the details of the case. When Bill included his photographs, and we worked in a few homey phrases, we'd have a completely different story than the other papers.

Three cups of coffee and four rewrites of my article later, I was back in the Toyota and on the road again toward the skyscrapers that were visible in the distance. Half an hour later, I was pulling into valet parking at the Biltmore.

The offices of Carleton Yang, under the name Jade Treasures Imports, resembled a larger version of Susan Wong-McCloskey's. The furniture was all mahogany, with carved dragon table legs and plenty of silk room dividers. The big difference was the enormous jade and ivory figurines displayed on equally impressive marble pedestals.

This was obviously not a working office, as the only filing cabinet belonged to the scintillating Chinese receptionist. She was right out of a James Bond movie. When she asked me to have a seat, I didn't care if Yang took the rest of the afternoon before meeting me, as long as I could sit with her in my view.

While I was waiting, she let me use the telephone to hook up my computer's modem and send my story to Bill. This way he could edit it and begin formatting the paper. I was sure he was going to make the story his front-page headline. Normally, I don't get very excited about a headline, but this time I wished I could see the faces of the people involved in the case when they read it. While I was at it, I e-mailed the story to the *Great Falls Tribune*. When our story came out, they were going to be inundated with telephone calls from Los Angeles. That should make their day.

Unlike my earlier impression of Sidney Lu, Carleton Yang was exactly what I had expected. He *did* look like Charlie Chan in a business suit. I placed him at about sixty. Again, though, my first impression was disappointing. Here was another guy who wouldn't know what was going on out in the street. However, I thought with a positive note, since he was in business for himself, he might be a Republican and, therefore, he might not mind digging up some dirt on the Democratic National Committee. Being an Independent, I didn't care if the dirt hit the Democrats or the Republicans, as long as it made good copy.

After shaking my hand, Mr. Yang got right to the point. "So. You want my help in finding out about that unfortunate situation in Palos Verdes a few days ago?"

I gave him the same story that I had given to Sidney, but added more. "The story looks like an assassination. If this were Chicago, I'd say it was a mafia hit. But this is Los Angeles, and the woman was Oriental."

This comment struck a cord!

Yang uncrossed his legs and leaned forward as he started speaking. "Orientals also have their mobs, as you call them. They are called Tongs and Triads. With the Asian population growing from roughly three and a half million to a projected twelve to fifteen million people in the United States by the year 2025, we, in the Asian community, can see better than anyone, the organized crime that comes with it. And, with LA being the preferred destination—we are projected to have at least 41% of the Asian and Pacific Islander population at that time. We feel it here more than anywhere else in the country."

He paused to catch his breath, re-crossed his legs, and then continued. "Just like the Black population, where black against black crime far outnumbers black on other ethnic groups, Asian Organized Crime, as the Director of the Federal Bureau of Investigation calls it, targets the Asian community. They extort protection monies, just as the Mafia did, or does. I don't know now.

"The Triads and Tongs are involved in drugs, extortion, alien smuggling, prostitution, loan sharking, murder, and all types of fraud. In fact, one of their biggest targets in the past has been exchange students from Hong

Kong and Taiwan. The student shows up with a new car, speaks limited English, and before long he's paying upwards of $10,000 a week just to avoid getting beat up. So you see, these monsters prey on whomever, and whatever they can."

The numbers he was throwing out at me got my attention. Al Capone in his hey-day never generated the money these people were making just going after college kids. I made a mental note that this would be a subject worthy of my attention when I got back home.

Yang went on. "In 1995, I attended a conference on Asian Organized Crime in Boston, where Louis Freeh, Director of the FBI, made a speech on the subject. You can get a copy of that speech over the Internet on the FBI's web page."

I had never expected a sixtyish Chinese exporter to be so with the times. Just goes to show you how little first impressions can mean.

"So," I said, "what you're telling me is that the murder, which looks like a mob hit, could be just that by a member of a Los Angeles gang?"

"Indeed. Which also implies that the murder victim could have been involved in something that wasn't entirely legitimate, or may have been the victim of extortion herself and was eliminated when she didn't pay up. There are an infinite number of possibilities."

"That's true," I replied. "But the type of execution still leads me to believe that it was a professional job. Because I'm bound by my word to the police, I can't tell you the exact details, but the killer left a distinguishing 'calling card' at the scene of the crime. In your nosing around, see if you can find any particular gang, or individual, that leaves a signature when they kill."

"Also, I don't know if the picture I told you about is anymore than just a memento of a one-time evening with the big boys. But, the more we can piece this woman's life together, the better chance we have of coming up with what was behind the killing, and that's where the story is."

I was carrying on a furious internal debate about the birth/ death certificate angle. I decided not to tell him for the time being. I could always call him in the morning and tell him about it then, after I'd thought it over some more.

Yang rose and extended his hand, giving me the not-too-subtle hint that the interview was over. I told him I'd be in touch with him within a day or two just to touch base. Walking with me to the door of the office, he told me to give him the weekend. If he had anything sooner, he'd call me.

More time to kill. It was a little after four and my next appointment wasn't until six. Time to make a call or two. I took the elevator down and crossed over to the Biltmore.

The Biltmore Hotel surprised me. I never expected gauche Los Angeles to have a hotel that ranked with the best of the East Coast and Midwest for opulence. The lobby spoke of quiet elegance rather than typical LA tacky.

I found a bank of telephones and called Bill. He had received my e-mail and was wild about the story, only he wanted more. I informed him more could be found in the last two issues of the *Daily Breeze* and *LA Times*. In addition, I told my anxious editor that we should be able to follow this blockbuster with one in each of the next two issues of the *Digest*. I made a bet that before the story ran its course, he'd increase his subscription readership by ten percent.

His response to this was, "Anything less than twenty won't pay for all the bills you're sending me. Are you lunching with every Oriental in town?" His chiding was only half in jest.

"Those that I'm missing for lunch, I'm picking up at dinner," I retorted. "So keep the ink wet in your pen."

After talking to Bill, I decided to take a walk around to see what the Los Angeles City center was like.

Directly across from the Biltmore looked to be a park. It took me exactly six minutes to find out that Los Angeles is like the false storefronts of an old Western movie set. It's all a facade. There's the Biltmore and a strip of buildings running two blocks deep and four blocks long. Beyond that strip there are more beggars, winos, pimps and prostitutes than in Chicago and Milwaukee put together.

I had no trouble finding Chinatown for my next appointment.

As soon as I saw Sun Fu Yee, I knew I had what I lacked with Lu and Yang—a person who would know what was going on out in the street. At least he looked the part. Sun Fu was dressed like a Chinese hood, complete with ponytail. He had on black pants, black sneakers and a black jacket with a dragon embroidered on the back. He was either the real thing, or headed the Hell's Angels Chinese fan club.

The restaurant wasn't exactly where you would take your date for a memorable Saturday night, unless you felt like experiencing the Chinese equivalent of the Mexican two-step.

It reminded me of a trip to Taipei that I had taken once. I had been told by a Chinese-American in our party that, if I ever wanted to eat there, I shouldn't look inside the kitchen. This was probably good advice to follow at the Mandarin Palace as well.

Despite my feeling that I was experiencing a time warp or had stumbled onto a Jackie Chan movie set, Sun Fu put me at ease. "How do you like my 50's look?" he asked. "That's the latest style around here. Pretty neat, huh?"

"Yeah, pretty neat. I don't think I ever felt more out of it than I do now."

"At night they don't get many tourists in this place," he said, "but during the day a few stray families exploring the back streets of Chinatown find their way here. Most of the tourist action is down the street where the arches are. What'll you have?"

"I had a big lunch not too long ago," I explained, "so just a beer. But don't let me stop you from eating."

"I'm just gonna have Low Mein."

The waiter arrived and Yee ordered for both of us in Chinese.

"So," he said, as the waiter walked away, "I understand you're looking for some help with the PV killing Sunday. Right?"

"Yeah, I'd like to find out a lot more about it."

By the time I'd finished outlining the situation for the third time that day, my beer and his Low Mein arrived. Good thing I didn't order anything to eat. There were no knives and forks on the table, just chop sticks.

"I've got good contacts around here," said Yee, after swallowing his first mouthful. "My guess is that it was a Triad killing, which means you're never going to find out who did it. Sometimes the pros are imported from either the mainland, Hong Kong, or Taiwan. They execute the contract and are on the way back the same day, disappearing from sight."

"That has to be a pretty expensive situation, with round trip air fare and expenses."

"Depends on how much you want the person dead," said Sun Fu, scooping up some more Low Mein. "No way are the locals gonna find the executioner to talk. It's very effective."

"So what you're telling me is, that the person who did the actual killing is probably long gone by now. Never to be heard of again."

"You got that right."

What he was telling me wasn't very encouraging, but it wasn't unexpected. Maybe because it was getting late, or I just felt like he wouldn't run to the *Times*, I told Sun Fu about the birth and death certificates. I explained that we needed to find out more about the fake Susan Wong and not to worry so much about who killed her, although I did mention the killer's calling card.

He assured me that he was going to work on it, and would probably have something before the weekend.

I believed him.

CHAPTER SIX

It was almost nine P.M. before I got back to the paper. My glasses still reflected the glow of all the headlights I'd faced on the drive back when Bill anxiously motioned me over to the table in the conference room to look at a proof of the story and layout of tomorrow's paper. It was great! He left my work intact with only a few minor changes, and integrated the less sensational facts of the case so that it all looked fresh. Even the pictures were great. He had a larger quantity of different angles than either the *Breeze* or the *Times*. He ended up devoting one entire page to the story.

"There hasn't been more space devoted to a killing on the front page since Kennedy was shot," said Bill.

"How do you know? We were both just kids?"

"There's a copy of the *Trib's* front page in our lobby."

We ceased our self-congratulations, called Bilbo, and asked him to come over. While we were waiting, I called McCloskey and told him that it was probably going to be a couple of hours, but I thought he should see what we were going to run. He said he'd wait up for me.

Bilbo was banging on the door as I hung up with McCloskey. He just nodded at me as he followed Bill to the table. I didn't bother to get up.

As he read the copy, Bilbo's blank facial expression

never changed. When he had finished he looked over at me and said, "I'm impressed." He turned to Bill. "The Chief isn't going to be very happy with this. I'm going to get my ass chewed pretty good for not coming up with this myself."

I felt like a turd, but war is hell.

He asked if he could use one of the offices to call his boss.

Bill guided him to his office and closed the door. "He's taking it pretty good."

"Yeah. Probably a lot better than you or I would. But there's not a helluva lot he can do about it"

Bill smiled, more to himself than to me. "I don't think I'll get invited to the Chief's birthday party this year."

"Were you last year?"

"Nope."

"So," I said, "you'll never know what you're going to miss."

Bilbo came out of the office. "The Chief wants me to bring him a copy."

"No can do." Bill covered the galleys. "We just can't take the chance that the *Breeze* will see this before they put their morning edition to bed. What good will it do for him to see it anyway?"

"You're right," Bilbo said, with a defeated shrug of his shoulders. "It's probably just a knee-jerk reaction. I'll just tell him that it's your working copy and you can't let it go. What time'll the paper hit the streets?"

Bill looked at his watch. "Our carriers will pick them up here at four in the morning. A half-hour later they'll start on their routes, and by five-thirty most will be delivered. You'll get your usual complimentary copy at the station between five and five thirty."

Bilbo turned his attention back to me. "Can I see the certificates?"

"They're on the way from Montana as we speak. As soon as they arrive, which should be tomorrow, I'll see that you get copies."

"How'd you find out about this?"

"I can't reveal my source. You know that."

He sighed. "What other surprises do you have in store for us?"

"Actually, Detective, none at the moment. But I'm working on it."

"I'm sure you are," he said. "But you'd better not be withholding evidence. This comes mighty close to it."

I disagreed, but let it lie.

"Look, Jeremy." He was heading for the door. "I've got to get out of here. I'll let you and Bill discuss the finer points."

I waved him a hand, knowing that I had to get to McCloskey's before Bilbo put everything together and came to the conclusion that McCloskey had to be the source.

Captain McCloskey opened the door before I knocked. "I've been waiting for you."

"Sorry I'm late, but we had to go over this with Detective Bilbo, so he wouldn't get too pissed when he reads it in the paper tomorrow."

He ushered me back to the same room we had talked in before. I took the same seat and proceeded to go over the story with him. He didn't interrupt. After I finished, he looked at me with the same bland expression that Bilbo had had. I'd never want to get into a poker game with those two.

At last, he responded with, "I don't know what to say. I had no idea. I think I told you once that I didn't know much about my wife's past when I married her." His tone of voice reminded me of a friend of mine who'd visited me one evening. He'd told me that his wife had just told him that she didn't want to be married anymore. He'd been like a blind person who couldn't find his cane.

I told him that Bilbo would probably put two and two together and figure out that he was the one who showed me the birth certificate. I told him not to lie. "Just tell him that you gave it to me. If he asks why, say that I asked if you had one, and that the police hadn't. Don't tell him that you volunteered it."

"I agree. That's the best way to handle it."

"Did your wife have a safe deposit box," I asked.

He shrugged his shoulders and said, "I don't know."

"I'll bet she did. From the things we've seen in the files, her bank was the Bank of Hong Kong. I think you should go there and find out."

"I don't have a key."

I told him that didn't make any difference and explained the procedure. "Under the circumstances, they'll want to see a death certificate and probably a court order. The court will insist that a police officer be present when you open the box. I don't know of any way around that unless you have an in at the bank."

"I don't know anyone at that bank. I do my banking at World Savings."

"When Bilbo comes to see you, talk to him about it. Say something like, 'I was thinking that my wife may have had a safe deposit box and maybe we should try and find

out where it is.' That should take his mind off the birth
certificate. Then volunteer that you believe your wife had
a business account at the Bank of Hong Kong. Say you
just want to know what's in it, okay?"

"Okay," he agreed, lighting a cigarette.

After my last visit, he must have figured out that was
the fastest way to get rid of me. I bid him adieu and left by
the side door. I wondered how long it would be before
Bilbo showed up.

Back in my car, I entertained thoughts of stopping by
the Brewery and looking for Lucinda, but given my state of
exhaustion, decided that bed was a more compelling
alternative tonight. I could devote some time to cultivating
my budding relationship with her sweetness tomorrow.

Thankfully, Bill didn't wake me up and show me the
paper. He left a copy on my nightstand so I wouldn't miss
it. When I did see the finished product, I still thought it
was a piece of work of which to be proud. I wasn't that
much of a factor in most of the editions at the *Trib*—just
one of many stories by one of many good reporters—so I
felt closer to this one. It was the first time I'd felt that I was
in the birthing room. It felt good.

What makes any reporter tick is the thought of his
story's impact. The one we just put out would make more
than a little wave, even in totally blasé Los Angeles. It
might even smoke out someone who knew something
about the killing. At least that's what I hoped it would do,
beyond putting Bill's paper on the map.

After congratulating one another the evening before,
I'd told Bill that, unless something unusual happened that
required my attention, I was not going to set foot in his

establishment today. He'd faked being hurt, but for what he was paying me, he'd told me to have fun and he'd left for the office without me this morning.

It wasn't long before I was on the phone to Lucinda. When I apologized for calling so early, she laughed. "I've run five miles, done a half hour of exercises, taken eleven vitamins, and I've already read your story, so you don't have to apologize for calling early."

"I'm taking today off and I'd like to monopolize you for the day." I didn't tell her that my exercise so far that morning had been sitting on the commode turning the pages of the newspaper.

"I'm not working until the evening shift," she said. "But I really don't want to get nearly killed again."

"I promise I'll make every effort to prevent that."

We agreed that I would pick her up in one hour. Back in Chicago, I would have specified an exact time, but "when in Rome do as the Romans do" was the rule. In Los Angeles, especially in the Beach Cities, between one and two hours is as exact as you're going to get.

Another thing I liked about this way of life was the way they sort of ease into a day rather than being whacked by it in the face.

As I started the easing on the patio, Bill called to inform me that he had already heard from the Chief of the Palos Verdes Estates Police, the Managing Editor of the *Breeze* who had called to congratulate him on the story, and one of the television networks asking for more information.

Bill also said that *Great Falls* had sent us a copy of their story, which was cross-complimentary. I could tell that Bill was trying not to sound like a college kid who'd just scored with the homecoming queen.

If I were on the payroll, this would have been a perfect time to ask for a raise. Instead, I told him that the receipts for my expenses were on my desk. In his current state of euphoria he wouldn't question anything. I probably could have given him a receipt for my evening with Lucinda and he'd have paid it.

I also asked Bill if he knew someone who could lift fingerprints. He said he didn't know of anyone off hand, but probably could find someone if we really needed it. I told him what I had in mind, then called McCloskey and asked him to bag a couple of his former wife's things, that she alone would have touched, and bring them to Bill. All I told the captain was I was playing on a hunch. He agreed to drop them off on his way to the Bank of Hong Kong to see if his wife had a safe deposit box.

My next call was to Carleton Yang. I asked him if he had connections with the authorities in Hong Kong. He said that the communist government kept most of the people in their old jobs after the takeover, so he still had sources. He agreed to send Susan Wong's fingerprints to see if they could make an identification.

The local law would send her prints to Washington, where they wouldn't find out anything. Washington would send them to Interpol, where they could have something, but, by that time, if my hunch paid off, we'd already have our information and another scoop. That triggered an adrenalin rush and really got me in the mood to see Lucinda.

When I saw her, I knew for a fact that the person who coined the phrase "look but don't touch" had never seen Lucinda in tee shirt and shorts, starting with the tee shirt—

just regular white cotton with a Miller's Beer Logo emblazoned on it—covering a firm set of mouth size little boobies. The palms of my hands were already twitching in anticipation of caressing those inviting morsels.

Quite naturally, my eyes flowed downward to her lithe hips, which bordered a tush that should be against the law. It made the little waitress at the sidewalk cafe look flabby. I could be sentenced to a jail term just for my thoughts, as I followed her down the steps.

Somehow I managed to get to the car without making a fool of myself. We'd decided to go to Laguna Beach for lunch. I didn't realize that it was a good hour and a half away, but time had flown by quickly with Lucinda stroking my leg while her lips had run up and down my fingers.

I had absolutely no idea how we had gotten to Laguna Beach, and lunch in a public restaurant wasn't exactly what I was in the mood for when we'd arrived. It didn't seem to faze her in the least that, by the time we got out of the car, I was sitting in a pool of sweat, panting like a half-crazed stallion.

My God, I thought. How can she think of eating at a time like this?

She didn't have any trouble at all.

We were seated at a window where we could see waves breaking over the rocks directly below us. It was idyllic and romantic, as if I needed more romance to get me in the mood. I had a hard time walking as it was. More romantic and I'd be stuck in my chair for the duration. In my condition, it wouldn't even be cost effective to get a motel room. If she just brushed by me, I'd be finished.

By the time lunch was over, I was calmer. It's amazing how a combination of Mahi Mahi and Chardonnay can mellow you. It seemed to have worked for Lucinda as well, only I wasn't sure that I wanted it to. I was mistaken. On the way back to the car, her hand found one of my most vulnerable spots—the back of my neck. When she started massaging the hair in that area, it drove me into a frenzy. Only one subject came to my mind—motel, and where to find one.

The little blue Toyota was transformed into a sleek red Ferrari as I zoomed out onto the Pacific Coast Highway heading north. The Travel Lodge near Newport Beach was the first motel that came into view.

As I pulled into the parking lot, the bundle of passion next to me asked, "What are we stopping here for?"

"What do you think?" I replied, my hand on the door latch.

"This isn't a very good time."

I was getting a little irritated. "Look, honey, you have me so I don't even need an engine to propel this car. It could go for miles just on the heat that I'm generating."

"I'm sorry," she said, moving closer to her side of the car. "But it's that time of the month, and it makes me a little passionate."

"A little passionate. Geez, I have a probe sticking out so far that I can probably refuel an airplane in flight."

She kissed me on the lips. "As soon as I get over my visitor we'll take care of that problem." She said that just before she sent a tongue probe into my mouth.

With the Toyota transformed back into a compact Japanese car, I got back on PCH heading toward the sanctuary of the South Bay. For my own sanity I changed the subject. "Tell me about the marketing job you had."

"Well, the company had a contract with a beer

company that wanted to sell more beer to the Hispanic market. Incidentally, Hispanics consume a lot of beer. My job was to present the cultural perspective to promotional campaigns primarily in the Los Angeles area." She elaborated by telling me further that the Hispanic market in Los Angeles was huge and getting larger.

"How huge is huge?" After hearing Carleton Yang's Asian numbers, I was genuinely interested in putting that in perspective.

"Let's put it this way. The Hispanic population in California alone is supposed to double by the year 2025 and account for at least one-third of the nation's total Hispanic population. In terms of people, Hispanics in California will be somewhere between sixteen to seventeen million. That's a lot of people."

I mentally added that to Carleton's number and came up with twenty-two million people, give or take a million. Anyway you cut it, it amounted to a pretty sizeable market for both beer and crime.

Lucinda was still talking. "Do you know that the Anglo population is staying pretty even, which means that whites will be less than half the population of California?"

I had to interrupt her to ask for directions. I had come up on a traffic circle and had no idea where I had to get off. After navigating through the maze, I turned my attention back to what she had said. When whites are less than half the population it would make interesting politics. "I wonder how those numbers will affect the country as a whole?"

"You have to factor in things like age, voting patterns, and such, to come up with anything half way meaningful," Lucinda replied.

"You're the one who's done the work on this. Educate me."

"Well, for example, most states are expected to have a decline in the proportion of people under the age of twenty. California will be one of the exceptions, and it'll show an increase in older people as well. Also, the white population tends to vote in greater numbers, so, unless the Hispanics and Asians begin voting, whites will continue to monopolize the government."

"You've put some work into this. I'm impressed."

She put her hand on my leg. The same leg that remained sensitive from the stroking it received earlier. "Part of my course work at USC, and looking at the census figures for my former job. I don't have much reason to use my brain in this way anymore. My waitressing clientele remain the same. Oversexed young men impressed with themselves and oversexed older men wanting a younger woman. What can I tell you?" She gave the inside of my leg a little pinch before removing her hand.

By the time we got home, we had just about solved the world's problems. Once again, I had to double-park, but the goodbye kiss was longer and much more inviting.

When I stepped inside Bill's, there was a note from him telling me to watch the local news. Sure enough, one of the lead stories was ours. We had done it. Not only had we scooped both the *Breeze* and the *Times*, we'd put Bill's paper on the map. We hoped the fallout would be the catalyst to rattle some of the bushes and drop something in our laps.

CHAPTER SEVEN

For the next two days, Bill had to chase his normal Peninsula stories. He covered a Junior League bazaar, an opening at the Norris Theater for the performing arts starring one of Hollywood's aging performers, and one of the many awards banquets for Realtors, where everyone is honored as a top producer so they can put it on their business cards.

I checked in frequently with the PV police department for anything new on the case. But, like me, they were awaiting information, though they were actively interviewing anyone they could find who had known the deceased.

Without a mole in the department, I was at the mercy of Detective Bilbo, who had become decidedly cool toward me. I had the feeling that his Chief didn't appreciate our beating the department to the birth\death certificate story.

The *Great Falls Tribune* informed me that they had a call from their local police department at the request of the Palos Verdes Estates police department about their part of the story.

The relationship between them and their upholders of law and order was on more solid ground. I was told that the Great Falls police were also digging into the records listing all deaths of people with Chinese ancestry over the past five years, so we abated our effort in that direction. I had a feeling that a request to the Social Security Department might follow to find out if the social security numbers of those people showed any activity.

They promised me the list as soon as they received it.

Other than that, I was resting, soaking up the sun, seeing Lucinda as much as I could, and generally doing what I came to Southern California to do—goof off.

My goof off period ended abruptly.

As I was watching the five o'clock news, one of Los Angeles' premier newscasters, whose sole claim to journalistic fame was a pretty face, good diction, and the ability to flawlessly read the monitor, announced, "We have a breaking story. Sidney Lu, a senior staff member in the city's Community Relations Department was murdered in front of his Chinatown apartment just hours ago. Police are now on the scene. We'll have more on this story as it unfolds. Mister Lu was a longtime aid of former City Councilman Mitchell Ling."

I immediately called Bill at the paper and told him.

"Jesus," said Bill. "You have a message on your voice mail from him. He said he mailed you something at the paper that you might be interested in and to call him as soon as you receive it."

"Bill, I've got a hunch that we might just be on to something that is a helluva lot bigger than we imagined. If Sidney's murder is related to the inquiries he was making for us, then we're playing with some pretty rough characters."

"You might well be right, Jeremy."

"That means we'd better start watching our backs a

little better."

"I agree," said Bill. "By the way, McCloskey called and wanted to talk with you."

As soon as I hung up with Bill, I called Stan in Washington to give him the news. His reaction was the same as mine. "Sorry to lose Sidney. He was a good source." That was the extent of his sympathy. "But you must be on to something big. I'll keep my eyes and ears open. Let me know if you get something that you need help from here, and let's touch base every other day or so."

My next calls were to Carleton Yang and Sun Fu Yee. I told them that Sidney Lu was doing essentially the same thing they were, and had landed in the morgue, so they'd better be very careful. I was walking a tight rope here. I wanted to warn them, but needed them both.

Neither was scared off. I got the impression that Yang had a nationalistic agenda that accounted for his help.

I couldn't figure out Sun Fu Yee's angle. Neither person had asked for payment of any kind. God only knows what their relationship with Stan was. As far as I knew, Stan was straight. Unless he was a closet switch hitter. But he had a wife and kids.

Yang's response was, "Very interesting. Don't forget to send me the woman's fingerprints so I can send them to Hong Kong."

Yee said, "Hey, this is starting to be fun, but don't forget yourself. Be careful."

That " don't forget yourself," was out of character from Yee's public persona, but I didn't say anything.

I called McCloskey. He told me that he had a couple of his wife's items for fingerprinting and wanted to drop them off. I told him to give them to Bill at the paper tomorrow, and to be sure they were in plastic bags. His next news floored me. "The travel agency office was broken into last night and all the files are gone."

"Have you called the police?" I asked.

"They called me. The manager of the Executive Suites discovered it when she came in, and she called the sheriff."

"Why the sheriff?"

"The sheriff's department has jurisdiction in Rolling Hills," said McCloskey.

"Oh, yes. I forgot. I have a heck of a time keeping all this straight."

"The sheriff's department called the PVE police who called me to ask if I knew anything about it. Now, why would they think I knew anything about it? I have a key."

"That's just the way they think. Remember, the spouse is always the prime suspect until proven differently."

"I remember, but I don't find it comforting. You don't believe I had anything to do with my wife's murder, do you?"

"Of course not. I'm on your side."

That seemed to reassure him. "I'll be glad when this thing is all over. The coroner won't even release the body for me to bury. It's like we're all in limbo."

I assured him with, "This isn't a run-of-the-mill heart attack we're dealing with here. The police move at their own pace and have a job to do."

"God, I hope so." I could hear the frustration in his voice. "I just want this nightmare to be over so I can get on with my life. Starting with sorting it over again."

This was the only advice I could give him. "You've got to take it a day at a time."

Then he dropped another bombshell. "We got a court

order to open my wife's safe deposit box at the Bank of Hong Kong. Bilbo had to be with me."

"And? Did you find anything interesting?"

"You might say that. We found over a hundred thousand dollars in cash, which the police took and gave me a receipt for."

All I could do was let out a whistle. "A hundred thousand dollars in cash." The IRS is going to have a field day with this."

After we hung up, I faced another dilemma. I had failed to tell McCloskey about the fact that I had a copy of his wife's files so, technically, I had taken them without permission. Also, Bilbo would have it out with me if he knew. I was sure he would consider it tampering with evidence and, given his feelings toward the *Digest*, we could expect some serious ramifications. On the positive side, there had to be something in those files that someone didn't want revealed. There was only one way to answer that question. The problem was, that most of the information was in Chinese.

There was only one way I could go. I had to trust either Carleton Yang or Sun Fu Yee to go over the files. My inclination was to call on Yee. I don't know why, but I just felt more comfortable with him.

I phoned Yee. He agreed to do it and said he'd meet me the next morning at the paper.

Bill called back to prod me for the story. Another edition of the paper was due and he needed my copy. We agreed to go with the break-in at the travel agency office as the lead story, hoping that neither the *Breeze* nor the *Times* would pick it up. No press release was issued by any of the law enforcement agencies on the matter, so it might slip through the cracks. I cranked up the laptop and started to write:

> The Office of U.S. Tours in Rolling Hills Estates was broken into late last night, and all files removed. U.S. Tours was owned and operated by the brutally murdered Peninsula resident, who assumed the identify of Susan Wong. Wong was a deceased woman from Great Falls, Montana.. The dead woman's identity remains a mystery.
>
> The murder is under investigation by the Palos Verdes Estates Police Department. This case continues to baffle the authorities who have failed to come up with either a killer or a motive. At the present time, there are no known suspects.
>
> This office burglary did not appear to be the work of amateurs. Other than the files, nothing was destroyed or vandalized. Sources have also confirmed that police have located and confiscated the contents of the victim's safe deposit box, but no further information has been forthcoming.

Bill would clean it up and fill in the balance of the story with information from our last edition.

Ordinarily, I would have confirmed the details with the police, but having the husband as my source was about as credible as it gets. I was probably over conscious of leaks to the *Breeze* and *Times*. Bill's small paper was still swimming upstream. This story should really have cemented our relationship with the PVEPD.

Next on my agenda was a little Hispanic lovely whom I was pursuing as adamantly as I was the Wong murder, but with more emotion. I still hadn't succeeded in worming my way into her apartment for any length of time, let alone her bed. She was definitely playing it right. I kept coming back.

I called her apartment. No answer. It shouldn't have bothered me, but it did. She wasn't working that night. She had a life besides me. We'd known each other only a week. She should just sit around and wait for me to call? The voice of reason said I'm over forty years old and not going to make a long-term commitment to this woman, so I should lighten up and stop acting like a teenager with a crush on the teacher.

I opened a beer, plopped on the couch and turned on "Law and Order."

The new day had started with one helluva beginning. Sun Fu Yee must get up on East Coast time. He was waiting for me at the paper when I arrived. "Where you been?" he chided. "It's practically time for lunch."

"Yeah, sure." I was still ticked from the previous night. "What did you do, sleep on the park bench out here last night?"

"You should try it sometime. This is rarefied air up here compared to Chinatown."

I took him inside the conference room and showed him the files. I confided in him about the situation, emphasizing that I would understand if this compromised his ethics.

He said, "Hey, you didn't know the files were going to be burglarized when you copied them, so I don't see that you did anything so bad." He started translating.

While I was with Yee, McCloskey had dropped off his wife's things. He had a compact and a leather wallet in individual plastic bags.

Bill arranged for a fingerprinting expert through his security service. His contact said to drop off the items as soon as we had them, but to call first, and he'd deliver the prints in a couple of hours.

Ten minutes later I was on my way down the hill heading toward Torrance. I located the security service's offices snuggled within a grove of eucalyptus trees. For the first time since I had arrived in Southern California, it started to rain—a rarity in the summer. During one of his Chamber of Commerce orations Bill had told me that it was common for them not to have rain from April through September.

As usual, when I approached the turn to the office I was in the wrong lane of traffic and had to go an extra block before making my left hand turn. Somehow I made it. I deposited the articles and returned to the paper. I was able to tuck the Toyota behind a slow truck going up the hill, leaving the left-hand lane to the parade of Mercedes heading back to their Peninsula sanctuaries.

When I returned, Bill was pacing the floor brandishing a large manila envelope. "I think it came."

Hearing the commotion, Sun Fu Yee came out of the conference room. "Something wrong?"

"No," I said. "Just Bill hyperventilating. A picture came from Sidney Lu, which may give us a clue as to what he was on to, and why he was killed."

I opened the envelope and took out an 8 x 10 black and white photograph of two Asian males. One was the same person in the travel agency wall photo. The other I'd never seen before. At first glance, there was nothing unusual. Both men wore business suits, were neatly groomed, and appeared to be about the same age. On the back of the photograph was the logo, "Don Lee's Studios," along with an address and telephone number.

"Do you know this place?" I asked Yee.

"I know where it is, but I'm not familiar with the photographer. You know? If Sidney Lu was killed because of this photograph, this guy Don Lee might be next in line."

"Let's give him a call," I suggested. "It might be a little awkward, but he has to be warned somehow."

Bill intervened. "He might think this is a crank call, or hang up and run to the police. Either way, we don't have much to tell him except a hunch."

"Let me talk to him," Sun Fu Yee interjected. "I'll talk to him in Chinese and just tell him that we'd like to see him about the photograph he gave to Sidney Lu. He'll be more receptive if I don't speak English."

We agreed, and Yee dialed the number that appeared on the back of the photo. He didn't get an answer, and no answering machine picked up.

I felt a knot in my stomach the size of a bowling ball. "I've got a weird feeling that maybe we should take a ride to this place. We have to talk with him anyway. Let's just run this through the copier and take the copy rather than the original, just in case."

The consensus was that Yee and I would go. Bill would stay here and get out his paper. He made us promise that we would call him to let him know that we were all right. He also made it clear that, if he didn't hear from us in an hour, he was going to call the LAPD.

"Make that two hours," Yee said. "It's going to take us at least an hour to get there, and double if there's an accident on the freeway or something."

Yee said he'd drive. When we got to his car, I understood why. He drove a BMW coupe, and took off down Crenshaw like the guys I was calling idiots less than an hour ago.

As we were flying low toward Chinatown, I asked Yee if he was coming across anything interesting in Susan Wong's files.

"It's too early to tell, except that I haven't found a pattern of anything. It's just names of people, and their passport numbers. I found an appointment book. Most of it didn't make any sense, but there was one entry every Thursday at 1:00 PM for the past six months that piqued my curiosity."

"What was it?"

"It was just, 'meet L'."

"I'd ask the husband about it," I said, "but I doubt if he would know anything. They led separate lives. Is there a way to match the incoming and outgoing passport numbers, and if they were the same person?"

"I didn't look at it that way," said Yee. "I think the best thing I can do is translate the files, then we can use the computer to enter each name and do some electronic sorting. That way we can play a bunch of 'what if' games and see if we can spot some logical patterns and match names."

I agreed that it was a good idea.

Listening to him talk, I was getting the distinct impression that there was a lot more to Mr. Sun Fu Yee than 50's garb and hip talk. He spoke like someone who was computer literate. By the way he handled the photograph situation, he was very astute when it came to crisis management. I made a mental note to talk to Stan about the man whom I was trusting, and whom I knew next to nothing about.

We drove the rest of the way in virtual silence, as he and every other driver on the Harbor Freeway concentrated on proving that the 55-mph speed limit continues to be a figment of bureaucratic imagination.

We'd just passed the city center and were easing onto the Hollywood Freeway when Yee exited onto surface streets. He stopped once to consult his Thomas Guide before maneuvering the BMW through a maze of side streets. When he came to a screeching halt in front of a small clapboard home, he proclaimed it to be the studios of Don Lee.

Both of us jumped out of the car and ran toward the front door. The house would have been right at home in the Midwest, with a full sized front porch. Yee didn't bother to knock, but tried the door. It was unlocked.

Immediately, it was clear that we were too late. The place was a shambles. Drawers were pulled out, books were out of bookcases. It had been thoroughly torn apart by someone who didn't care in the least about disguising their activity.

"Jeez," Yee said. "This place is really a mess."

"Let's hope the owner wasn't here during their visit."

I went into the back room. "He's in here," I called to Yee. Lying on the floor in the middle of what would have been a dining room was a man's body.

"Is he dead?" Yee asked.

"I don't know." I turned the body over on its back. I

barely kept myself from throwing up. The face was a mass of torn and bloody skin. Dried blood from multiple cuts was caked on a full white beard. Two teeth fell to the floor from between swollen lips. When I forced myself to take a closer look, I thought I saw the man's chest heave a couple of times. "He's alive!"

Yee felt for a pulse. "You're right, he's got a pulse. Weak, but it's there." He dropped the arm and looked around the room. "I've got to find a phone."

We scurried around.

"Let's just call 911 for help and get the hell out of here," I suggested. "I don't know about you, but I don't feel like answering a lot of questions that I don't have answers to right now."

"You got that right," Yee said as he charged into the front room. "I found one," he yelled.

"Make sure you don't touch anything." I was not too far behind him.

Covering his hand with his handkerchief, Yee used a pen to punch 911. After giving the operator the number of the house and the nature of the problem, we jumped back into the BMW and headed for the freeway.

"I sure hope some concerned citizen didn't get your license number back there," I said.

On the way back, I reflected on what had been happening. I had started this thing by seeing a dead woman. Now I felt responsible for the death of Sidney Lu, the possible death of a person I didn't even know, and I'd placed Carleton Yang and the man beside me in jeopardy. I debated about telling Bill that enough is enough.

Yee must have been reading my thoughts. "You can't go blaming yourself for this. Whoever did this would have eventually done the same thing when the police got around to checking on the original photograph. The same photographer took both of them."

I still didn't feel much better. "You might be right when it comes to the photographer. But that's not the case with Sidney Lu. If I had left it to the police, he wouldn't have been involved."

"True," replied Yee. "But Mister Lu could have declined to help you. You didn't force him, just as you aren't forcing me to help you."

"I'd understand, though, if you wanted to cut your losses right now and get out of this mess."

"Not on your life," he said. "I want to see this to the end. I don't like people who do what I just saw, and I'd like nothing better than to get rid of their kind." Yee started to sound like Carleton Yang. "From what I know about this case, we're dealing with people who are endangering my people. I'm helping you because I want to stop this shit before it gets to be like the Mafia was in your hometown back in the twenties and thirties."

"You don't happen to know Carleton Yang, do you? I ask because you sound like him."

"Yes, I know of Mister Yang."

"What's your connection?"

He evasively replied. "Our paths have crossed."

"How do you know Stan Wasnewski?"

"I've done some favors for Stan, and he's done some for me in the past."

"I didn't know Stan's job took him to the West Coast," I said.

Yee smiled. "Stan told me when he called that you were good and asked me to cooperate with you. Let's say that LA isn't exactly the colonies, and Washington the mother country.   There is more campaign money funneled from LA to politicians in Washington than any other place in the union, including New York. Hollywood actors are greater contributors to the Democratic Party than anyone else in the country. Not only do they kick in bucks on their own, they donate their personalities, which brings in money by the bushels. Also, the Republicans don't exactly come off as the Little Sisters of the Poor here. Ronald Reagan, for example, had enough pledges from his Hollywood brethren to finance his initial dive into the political arena."

"To do his job in Washington," I said, "Stan has to have eyes and ears in Los Angeles. Is that what you're telling me?"

"Yes," he replied, pointing to the houses adjacent to the freeway that were visible from the car. "So, in addition to praying that we don't stall here right in the middle of Watts, let's just go along and finish what we've started. Now we know we're not up against a bunch of boy scouts, so let's watch our asses."

I just couldn't let it lie there, so I asked, "Who do you believe is behind all of this? And do you think that there's a tie between the contributions to the Democratic party and the murder of Susan Wong?"

Given that Stan had spent a lot of time working on that story, Yee telling me that he did some West Coast snooping for Stan, the photograph found in Susan Wong's office, the photograph uncovered by Sidney Lu, and the mauling of the photographer who took the pictures, it looked like there was a connection.

"This whole thing smells Tong or Triad," said Yee.

"But, like you, I don't know why or how. The killing of the woman in Palos Verdes was typical, and it isn't mere coincidence that Sidney Lu was silenced when he found something he wasn't supposed to."

He paused as he glided the Beemer through a freeway interchange. "The photograph is something else again. Someone didn't want that photograph in circulation, and Lu knew who, but was killed before he had a chance to tell you. I don't think the photographer knows anything, but was just in the way when someone broke in. I think he was taking pictures at the fund-raiser and caught someone on film who didn't want to be photographed."

"It has to be the other person in the picture,"

"Right. And I don't know who that is. You should send the picture to Stan. He's got some good sources."

He was right. The picture was taken at a Democratic fund-raiser and, if the person in the picture was a large contributor, someone might recognize him.

Yee dropped me off at the office and returned to Chinatown. Before I went home, I overnighted a zeroxed copy of both photographs and the fingerprints to Stan, asking him if he knew someone in the FBI who would see if they could recognize anyone, and check on the prints.

I had my hand on the doorknob ready to exit the building when the next brilliant idea hit me. Turning around, I called Carleton Yang. He was still in his office and agreed to send a copy of the photograph, along with the fingerprints, to his contacts in Hong Kong. I persuaded one of Bill's staff to stick around until a messenger service could take it to Yang that same evening.

CHAPTER EIGHT

The next time I called Lucinda, which was as soon as I got home, she picked up the phone on the second ring.

"I've been trying to reach you," I said.

"You've succeeded."

The ball was in my court. The only thing I could do was ask her out for dinner.

She replied that she had to go to work at six and wouldn't be off until midnight, and then all she wanted to do was go to bed and sleep. She asked me to go running with her the next morning.

Yeah, I thought, I'd get to the end of the block before dropping dead. "Why don't I go walking with you and save myself from a cardiac arrest?"

"OK, let's meet in front of my place around six. I have to get ready for work. See you in the morning."

The line went dead before I had a chance to say anything else. I got the impression that I was not exactly in control of this relationship.

I wasn't in the mood to sit and watch television. That's not what I came to Southern California to do. In fact, I wasn't doing anything that I'd planned to do in Southern California.

The phone call and semi-brush-off by Lucinda put me

in a rebellious mood. *I'll show them. The hell with Bill's chicken breasts. To hell with Lucinda's fish. To hell with all the God damned health freaks who drink carrot juice spiked with celery and go to health clubs. To hell with running on the beach everyday with their strangling spandex snuggled around tight little butts. To hell with all the wine drinkers of this stupid world.*

I decided to live dangerously and have some rare red meat dripping with blood and a Budweiser, instead of Corona with a stupid lime hanging out of the opening so you can't even get a man sized gulp.

While driving, I noticed a restaurant called The Bull's Corral in the Riviera Village that seemed perfect. Not only that, there was a Baskin Robbins right next to it. Red meat wasn't going to be my only source of perversion, I could have a chocolate sundae made with real ice cream for dessert. My arteries were going to stand up and salute from this double fat whammy by the time this night was over.

The Bull's Corral was just what I'd expected. No pretensions here. I was in for a good old Midwestern style cholesterol food fest.

The hostess led me to a booth at the end of the dining room, adjacent to the bar. I ordered rare roast beef, mashed potatoes with gravy, and salad with chunky blue cheese dressing and a Budweiser on draft. The waitress brought bread and real butter along with my beer. This was living! And the best part was, there was no one around to give me that disapproving holier-than-thou-smirk. Every once in awhile it felt good just to be able to be me.

The roast beef was savory. I could taste the warm blood in every mouthful. I raised my beer in a silent tribute to the valiant steer that so gallantly gave his life so others, like me, could enjoy his supreme sacrifice. I devoured every morsel, then soaked up the juices left on the plate with a piece of white bread heavily laden with rich creamery butter. I washed it down with cold Bud.

Leaning back in the booth, I observed the patrons of the Bull's Corral. They definitely weren't your stereotypical Southern Californians. I'm not good at guessing ages, but it looked to me that everyone was between the mid-fifties and death-by-morning.

There also seemed to be an inordinate amount of single women sitting at the bar. Not hookers, but a bunch of lonely widows and divorcees too young for the old folk's home and too old for Hennessy's.

I wondered if the place's name was the result of the food they served or the service they provided. I've heard of places like this being called middle-aged meat markets. I really didn't care. I wasn't in the mood to perform a civic duty and hit on a widow or divorcee, so I paid the check and left.

After I ate, it was still fairly early. So, with nothing else on my social calendar, I decided to drive the short distance to the Esplanade and watch the sun set.

There was one thing I found out while I was sitting in my car watching El Sol disappear towards Hawaii—it's not something someone who's feeling lonely should do. The other thing I realized was that when you're in the middle of a Midwestern prairie, twilight doesn't take on the same finality as sitting on the western edge of the continent watching that fireball disappear over the contrasting blue waters of the Pacific Ocean.

When the last rim of brightness had disappeared, it was

still too early for bed and I didn't feel like heading to any of the numerous local watering holes. Maybe it was the maudlin mood I found myself in that created the twinge of guilt that I felt about Bill and his staff laboring late at night to get out the next morning's edition of the *Palos Verdes Digest*. The next thing I knew, I was headed back up to the hill to give Bill a hand.

The lights were burning almost as brightly as the setting sun when I pulled the Toyota into the parking lot. Inside, Bill was peering over the computer, setting his copy, when I pulled a chair up beside him and said, "Need a hand?"

Bill smiled. "Always able to use some extra help if the price is right."

He proceeded to give me enough to do until well past midnight. Only then, did I realize what I'd been treating in an off-handed way meant to my friend. This paper was his profession, his marriage, his family, and his mistress. It had become his total reason for being.

The dream and the fantasy were realized with every issue that hit the street. It was like being present at the birth twice a week. I wondered if I would ever find anything as complete. It also made my situation with Lucinda so damn insignificant. I almost wanted to stick my finger down my throat and regurgitate the evening's meal.

When the paper was put to bed, I felt the same sense of accomplishment and pride that Bill was feeling. The next morning people would wake up, open the news to read the latest in the death on their hill, and not even realize that a faceless Sidney Lu had died, or that Bill and his staff had worked almost all night to bring them that bit of trivia. Nor would they care.

For the first time since I arrived in Southern California, I was out of bed before Bill, thanks to a God awful six am date with Lucinda. I was pretty proud of myself. And I was only fifteen minutes late.

She saw me valiantly hunting for a parking space and motioned for me to pull into the alley behind her building. Heretofore I wasn't informed that there was parking there. *I must be making progress*. But I knew that was a stupid mistake as soon as I thought it. She just didn't want to wait for me while I circled another three or four times.

The running shorts I'd put on for my morning's foray into this alien world made me feel as uncomfortable as a virgin in the Clinton White House.

My white legs were attached to a posterior that had succumbed to the earth's gravitational pull. It was obvious that I stood out in startling contrast to the firm buttocks and tanned legs of the local fanatics.

There's nothing like trying to impress the girl you want to succeed with. I felt like a sideshow. Though I could suck in my stomach for an inordinate amount of time and carry that off pretty well, I couldn't keep my rear end from sagging. I supposed I could walk with a hand under each cheek, but that would have become a little awkward.

I decided to let things fall where they may, yet, making sure that Lucinda never walked behind me. As we started our walk, I discovered very quickly that I need not have worried. She took off like a mechanical rabbit at a greyhound park, and I was left in her rear doing my best to keep up.

"Let's walk to PV," she said, turning south."

My immediate thought was that they called PV "the hill" for a reason. "I've never been north?" I countered, noting that it was all level ground that way. "Why don't we go that way?"

"O.K." She did a quick pirouette without seeming to break stride. "We can walk to Hermosa."

If memory served me correctly, Hermosa Beach is after Redondo Beach and we were still in Torrance. "How far is it to Hermosa?" I asked, hoping humor would disguise my terror when I heard the answer.

"Oh, it's only three or four miles. We'll follow the bike path." She started down the steps from the sidewalk to the bike path. The path paralleled both the sidewalk and the ocean, with about thirty yards of sand in between. Calling it the bike path was a misnomer. It served roller skaters, rollerbladers, and pedestrians as well as bicyclists going in both directions, on four feet of concrete. There was no such thing as a leisurely stroll, but a massive game of chicken with no winners. Bill had told me about some of his close calls with women running while pushing baby strollers.

All I needed to complete my humiliation in front of Lucinda was for him to come tooling by and make some outrageous comment such as, "Watch him closely. We don't know how he might react in fresh air."

By my dogged determination not to let my male ego get in the way of common sense, I managed to set the pace, slowing my companion down to a more modest pace that fit my physical condition. After the Laguna Beach incident, and what I perceived to be her general attitude lately, I concluded that I had stumbled across the ultimate controlling PT which, back before the liberating 90's, was short for prick teaser. These got you all hot and bothered and then left you to lift the back of a car to relieve the pain in your groin. Until recently, I'd thought all PT's had become ancient history, having disappeared into the world of the PTA, minivans and soccer practices.

It was either that, or she'd gotten advice about baiting a man until he wanted you so badly that he'd do anything to get you, including marriage. Or maybe she'd been listening to her priest, one of those celibate marriage advisors, who'd convinced her that having premarital relations was sinful.

One thing was for damn sure, if my physical relationship was going to be confined to getting up at five thirty in the morning to dodge bikes and skaters so I could spend the rest of the day recuperating from all the exertion, I was going to try my sexual luck elsewhere. At this point, I didn't care that she was one of the sexiest looking women I'd come across in a long time. Being physically exhausted to be sexually deprived just wasn't worth it.

We made it to the Hermosa Beach pier without a problem. It was a pleasant walk once Lucinda understood the ground rules—meaning I was going to walk, not run— although I did manage to accelerate the pace once I made my point. After a brief rest, I resisted the urge to call a cab to take us back, and managed to get back to Torrance Beach without needing an oxygen tank.

Lucinda asked me in for some juice. She didn't drink coffee in the morning. We'd no sooner gotten up the stairs into the apartment when she grabbed me and made me the recipient of one of the most passionate kisses I can ever remember having. If what followed is an example of Latin desire, I wanted more of the same. My running shorts were all but ripped off. Hers followed mine to the floor.

We were still standing there naked, except for my

sweat socks that I couldn't get off without extracting myself from Lucinda's clutching embrace, when she jumped up and encircled my waist with her legs, still kissing me with reckless abandon. I didn't know what brought this on, and cared even less, as my eyes were searching the room for a place to lie down without resorting to the floor. Her bedroom beckoned from across the room. The door was open and I could glimpse her bed from where we were standing.

I delicately made my way across the room, still carrying Lucinda. It was the adrenalin mixed with an injection of testosterone and an underutilized libido that carried the day, and I made it.

My next hurdle was stooping over to lay Lucinda on the bed without my knees collapsing or my back breaking. Once that had been accomplished, she was in a perfect position for me to forget about any further foreplay, so I could do what I'd been wanting to do since we'd met. Mission accomplished. What a ride! She was as active as a mechanical bull set on expert. The bed rocked from one end of the room to the other. One can only wonder how we would have demolished the room if I had lasted longer than it takes to pour a cup of coffee. The first time is just the preliminaries before the main event anyway.

Over the next two hours, I demonstrated my stamina and recuperative powers twice more to Lucinda. They weren't exhibitions in room demolition, leaning more toward my finesse style than brute strength. She didn't complain!

It was almost noon before I dragged myself to the paper.

Bill greeted me apologetically. "I must have overslept this morning. You were gone before I even woke up."

"I went for a walk along the beach with Lucinda."

"You'd better be careful. You don't want that fresh air to get to you. But you did better than I did this morning. I didn't even have my morning bike ride."

"By the way, Bill. Where do you go riding most of the time?"

" I ride on the Peninsula. Why?"

"I just wondered. We walked along the bike path along the beach and it was like you said, we were dodging as much as we were walking."

"The only people who use that path are either those who can't ride on hills or those who want to impress the girls. The varying terrain on the Peninsula makes it more challenging, and keeps you in better shape. So, now that you know where to ride, when will you decide to take up the sport?"

"You'll be the first to know. And that won't be until they make more comfortable seats."

"Oh," said Bill. "Before I forget. Detective Bilbo called this morning about our story. He sounded a bit perturbed that we knew about the break-in at the travel office. In his opinion, we're walking a thin line printing stories like that without calling for corroboration."

"Yeah, sure," I replied. "Call him for corroboration. That just gives him a chance to try and bully us into not printing stuff. Just think how perturbed our friend Bilbo would be if he knew we had the files, and that we could tie Sidney Lu's death in with this one?"

"Anyway," Bill continued, "he said if we knew anything more about it, he'd appreciate us coming forward.

Maybe we should come clean about the files. After all, you had permission from McCloskey."

I reminded him that I had McCloskey's permission to look at them, not to take them off the premises and copy them. Then I inquired, "Has Sun Fu Yee been back?"

"Not today, yet," said Bill. "But the files are still in the conference room. Maybe we should take a look at what he's done so far."

Yee had gotten further than I'd thought. Now I was even more anxious to find out what made them so valuable. I asked Bill what spreadsheet programs he had on his computers. Luckily he had Quattro Pro, which I was somewhat familiar.

We settled down with the laptop and started to work. Since I won the fastest typist contest by acclamation, Bill read off the individual names. By the end of the hour we had one year's tours all neatly assembled on the spreadsheet, and I'd even remembered to save the data. Bill suggested that we make a copy on a floppy before printing.

Bill put the floppy on his desk to take home. He took the printout and placed it in the file cabinet in his office. This was probably a good example of overkill, but, with the travel office being burglarized, Sidney Lu getting murdered, and the photographer getting mauled and his place searched, we had to be careful.

We didn't have much—only a bunch of names and dates. It wasn't until Bill started going over the copies of the airline ticket folders that we found the answer to our dilemna. International tickets always have coupons for the entire journey as part of the packet, and during my first pass through the files, I had assumed that was all they were and hadn't examined them thoroughly. Bill examined each copied item in detail and found several tickets with unused return vouchers. In each tour group there had been at least two, and up to four, people who had entered the country and who'd never left. Also, the missing had never showed up.

"I'll bet that when we look at the other years," I said, "we find the same thing."

"It only takes an hour a year," Bill said "Let's do it."

We did it, and discovered that as the years progressed, the number of unaccountable people per tour group increased. "It was like they were running a pilot project," Bill said. "As they worked out the bugs, the groups became more frequent and the people more numerous."

The pieces started to fit. Get into the country, get an identity from someone who has just died, take over their social security number, get a new driver's license, register to vote at the same time, and bingo, you've just become a U.S. citizen. The only way you could possibly be caught is if the real person had his or her fingerprints on file from being in the service, applying for a security clearance, or serving prison time.

"So, it looks like our mystery lady was involved in alien smuggling, and we can't say anything about it without going to jail for obstruction of justice," Bill lamented.

"It's only one more piece of the puzzle," I reminded him. "There's still more. Who's in the picture that got Sidney Lu killed? Why was I run off the road for following someone from a restaurant? And the big one—who killed Susan McCloskey?"

"Still," Bill said, "it's a shame we can't use this. What

a story it would make."

Just then, Sun Fu Yee called to say that he wouldn't make it in today.

I told him what we'd discovered.

"Man, we're really on to something here," he said. "This opens up all sorts of avenues."

"Or blind alleys," I replied. "It also makes the original death here on the hill seem like an amateur playing in a high stakes game."

"I think we've already seen evidence of that."

"Yeah, which reminds me. Have you heard anything about the condition of our photographer?"

"That's where I've been all morning. It seems he's regained consciousness and will be fine when his bruises heal. The police aren't treating this any different than they would any break-in. At least there's no guard or anything outside his hospital door. I walked right in."

I was astounded. "You actually talked to him?"

"Yep," said Yee. "Sure did. He told me that he was working when two Chinese men walked in and wanted to see all his pictures from the fundraiser. Because of what he'd given Sidney Lu, he was immediately on guard and told them he had disposed of all that a long time ago. He said one of the men punched him and the last thing he remembered was lying on the floor being kicked."

"I guess he wouldn't know if they found anything?"

"I asked him that," said Yee, "and he said they wouldn't have found anything because nothing was there."

"Would he tell you what happened to all of his negatives?"

"Even though I convinced him that I was a friend of Sidney's, he wouldn't say where they were or if they even existed."

Yee's call reminded me that I needed to touch base with Stan about the pictures and fingerprints overnighted by Federal Express. Due to the three-hour time difference, I called his cell phone.

"Yeah, I got everything and the picture is already circulating. It'll be a couple of days. On the prints, unless they're from someone with a criminal record, we might strike out. However, my friends in the Bureau told me that if they don't have a match, they'll send them to Interpol to see if they have anything."

Once again, Stan's cooperation amazed me. We hadn't ever been bosom buddies, and since I wasn't even working on a story for the *Trib*, I wondered why everyone was being so damned nice and cooperative. I didn't usually get such service from anyone when I was pursuing a story. All of this buddy-buddy stuff made me cautious, so I didn't volunteer the information Bill and I had gotten from the files.

It was well into the afternoon and I was getting hungry. Evidently Bill's stomach was telling him the same thing, because he asked me if I'd like to get something to eat. He knew where we could get the best fish in town for the lowest price. I told him to lead on. After my red meat pig-out the previous night, I felt guilty enough for fish.

Once again Bill was right. We ended up at a place called The Seafood Broiler, which looked like the old Victoria Station chain where the restaurant was actually several old railroad cars placed end to end.

For less than five dollars, excluding tax and beer, I had a great meal of fresh Idaho trout, my favorite fish, with rice pilaf, cooked veggies, and coleslaw. Excluding my dinner with Lucinda, talking old times with Bill over this fine meal was the best time I'd had so far in California. Ever since I'd arrived, we had been obsessed with the case and, even though we shared the same living quarters, we hadn't had time to really sit down and talk.

Bill confided that he missed married life, and still thought of his former wife quite a bit. Not only was she re-married and living in Birmingham, Michigan, she was totally installed in local society, belonging to all those organizations that he wrote about in his paper, like the Junior League and ladies country club golf.

"She loves it," Bill said. "She realized she wouldn't have it with me. I'm too busy chasing my dreams. How 'bout you? How do you feel about your own divorce? Do you ever see Rita?"

I was honest when I said, "A person couldn't share the things we shared and not remember all the good times we had. But I have no intention of ever getting married again. I don't need anything to complicate my life. Like you, I'm happy doing the kind of work that I do."

"Are you going to stay with the *Trib*?" asked Bill. "And be an investigative reporter for the rest of your life?"

That wasn't as easy an answer to give. I admitted to my friend that I had been thinking of leaving the paper for some time to do freelance work, similar to what I was doing for him. "I find myself limited to what I can cover there," I elaborated. "I'd like the freedom of picking my own stories without restraints. The only problem is, I have to earn money for the basics, like food and shelter."

Bill made me an offer that I knew I would have to seriously consider.

"Tell you what," he said, "the spare bedroom is yours

116

for as long as you like. If you want to go off on your own, you can live here with me. The only thing I would ask is for you to give me a hand once in awhile, should something come up like we're working on now."

I thanked him for his offer and promised to think about it. Something like this always seems to happen. I spilled out my guts and Bill's offer forces me to make a decision. You just can't win.

Lunch and a couple of beers later we both decided to call it a day, and we did something that neither of us had done in years. We went to an early movie.

CHAPTER NINE

The next three days were devoted to pleasure. One day was dedicated to Lucinda and carnal gratification in her apartment. We made love four times. Luckily she had to work that night and I could drag my wasted body back to Bill's. With her sexual appetite, I would have had to perform at least once more, and that could have spelled the end of me. But what a way to go. It was going to be a helluva habit to break when I had to go back to Chicago.

On the evening of the third day, after a rigorous afternoon on Bill's patio reading a good book while devouring junk food and drinking beer, Bill told me that Carleton Yang had called and asked that I meet him in his office the next day. He suggested ten in the morning and to call only if I couldn't make it. My decadent lifestyle was coming to an end.

At 10:02 the following morning, I was ushered into Carleton Yang's office where two others were already present. Yang motioned me to an empty seat and introduced the others as Messrs. Chen and Teng. They stood and shook my hand, nodding a silent greeting.

Yang explained, "Mr. Chen and Mr. Teng have just flown in from Hong Kong. They have an interest in the

119

case that you are following. I have taken the liberty of telling them everything I know, but obviously you know more about it than anyone else, including the authorities."

I wasn't about to tell them anything more until I found out who and what they were, and said so. "May I ask what your interest is in the case?"

Yang nodded his head slightly and answered for them. "Of course." He then proceeded to tell me that Mr. Chen and Mr. Teng were officials of the Chinese Government. They were former members of the Hong Kong police anti-crime division who had been commissioned by the new government to continue their investigation into Triad and Tong activities in the province.

Listening to this bizarre turn of events, my mind went into warp speed. It was more than just coincidence that these two came here as soon as the picture and the fingerprints were sent. I addressed the two visitors. "I take it that the people in the picture and the fingerprints are the reason you're here?"

Again Yang replied for them. "Yes, that is the reason they are here."

While he was talking, I looked closely at the two men from Hong Kong. Mr. Teng was the older of the two by maybe ten years. I placed him in his late fifties to early sixties, although he didn't have gray hair.

One statement I could make with absolute certainty— they both went to the same barber. Their haircuts were identical. Neither had sideburns, and there was no attempt at tapering to form an eye pleasing transition from the top of the head to the sides. There was no effort to disguise where scissors stopped and razor began. They were both clean-shaven. In fact, it didn't look like either one of them ever had to shave.

By the fit of their suits, the first thing the Communist government must have done after they took over the territory, was eliminate all the good tailors and replace them with prison labor. Granted, they'd just had a long flight, but not even sleeping in the same clothes for thirteen or fourteen hours could account for the fit. Chen's collar resembled a Columbo knock off. Both were candidates to make Mr. Blackwell's worst dressed list.

It was obvious I wasn't going to be told anything until I spoke my piece. So I started at the beginning and told them everything I knew about the case, including the files. Carleton interrupted me at infrequent intervals to translate some of the slang that I'm prone to use.

When I was done, I looked directly at the two Chinese visitors. "Now that I've told you everything that I know, I would appreciate reciprocation."

I knew they understood me because both of them nodded their assent. However, it was Yang who explained that he had known the two for many years and had worked with them on occasion when Hong Kong was under British control. They had kept in contact after the transfer of power from the British to the Mainland Chinese government. Because of this contact, he had sent the information that he received from me to them. He said that they had immediately recognized both men in the picture, but only one was of interest to them. Our mystery man.

No surprises yet, although I have to admit I was sitting on the edge of my chair listening as the story unfolded. They also told me what had been in the back of my mind since Sidney's death. The mystery man was a notorious

Triad leader from Hong Kong who had disappeared several years ago, but they thought he was still behind much of the smuggling and drug traffic in the province. He continued to be at the top of their version of the FBI's most wanted list.

Yang said that the United States authorities hadn't been alerted that Chen and Teng were here. This tidbit of information suggested to me that, should they locate the Triad leader, they intended to either smuggle him back to China or flat out eliminate him. They were satisfied to know that their man was a criminal, and more than willing to use instant justice in handling the situation.

I told them I was sorry, but at the moment I had no idea where they could find their man. Lurking in the back of my mind, however, was a hunch about where he could be found.

When they got around to the fingerprints, they did surprise me. This time Teng did the talking. "It seems that the prints of the murdered woman, Susan Wong-McCloskey, match the prints of our Triad leader's mistress, who disappeared when they lost track of him. We didn't think anything of it at the time, because it wasn't anything unusual. Her turning up as the wife of someone else is what surprised us."

The one thing they knew for sure now that they knew she had a new identity, was that the Triad leader also had been given a new identity, for all the good it would do us. Talk about the proverbial needle in a haystack. All we had to do was find out the name of some Chinese man who died somewhere in the United States who was approximately the same age as our Chinese Triad warlord at the time he dropped out of sight. Even in this wonderful age of electronic information, we needed more than that. The Chinese government must have wanted this guy awfully badly to send two detectives here with such lousy odds.

When I voiced that thought, Teng said, "We realize that, but believe if you publish what you know in your newspaper, it will, as you say, 'smoke him out.'"

Oh, great, I thought. Sidney Lu can move over. I'm sure he'd love to have company wherever his spirit now resides.

I was getting stiff just sitting, so I got up and moved around a little. I didn't know if this was the right protocol or not, but did it anyway. Carleton also got up and asked if any of us would like some refreshments. I thought they would ask for tea, being Chinese who lived and worked for the British most of their lives. They didn't. They asked for coffee. Yang buzzed his receptionist.

I started something. The two Chinese detectives also stood up.

I turned to Teng and continued with my thought. "What you're saying is that our friend will want to find out where I'm getting my information and then, perhaps, silence me. I'll go to great lengths to get a story, but I don't relish the thought of joining Sidney Lu."

"That, of course, is your decision," Yang replied as he rejoined us.

At no time during the entire conversation did the two Chinese visitors betray their thoughts with body language or facial expressions. When they sat, they sat passively. When they stood they stood just as passively, arms at their sides, wearing blank expressions.

I have never considered myself a candidate for

martyrdom, but this was shaping up to be one helluva story. My only concern was that I was so vulnerable. The Triad played for keeps. I had to admit, it got me thinking rash things like Pulitzer Prize.

We had intended to pass on a story for the next edition of the *Peninsula Digest*, which was due out the next day (Saturday), but that was before this meeting. It would be awfully hard not to print what I had just heard.

While I was thinking, Carleton was talking. "We would like to keep Mr. Teng's and Mr. Chen's visit a secret for the moment, but that should be no problem because you are not obligated under law to reveal your sources." It was a statement rather than a question.

They were banking that my ego wouldn't allow me to not print the story, and they were right. I hate it when people prey on a person's weaknesses, particularly when they're mine. They damn well knew, and they knew I knew they knew, that I was going to print the story. I'd be lucky if it was only the Triads that would try to kill me. I might be better off with them than with Detective Bilbo after he read the next edition. I made a mental note to talk to Bill about it being time to take Bilbo into our confidence. I might need some police protection before this thing was over. It was taking on a life of its own and I was being swept along in the tide.

My thoughts were interrupted and the conversation halted when the door opened and two young women, one I recognized as the receptionist from the outer office, entered with trays of coffee. The remainder of the meeting was filled with meaningless chitchat while we finished our beverage.

Before I left, I told them that I would think about their

proposal and get back to them. I was anxious to get back to the Peninsula. I had a story to write.

Bill had been as nervous as a whore in church waiting for me. It may have seemed cruel of me not to have stopped and called him. However, I didn't have a cell phone, there aren't a lot of places along the freeway to make telephone calls, and given the neighborhoods along the Harbor Freeway, discretion had been advisable.

He ushered me into his office before I had a chance to use the facilities. By the time I was through telling him what had happened, he was fidgeting. I could see him struggling with the decision to print the story. "I can't let you jeopardize your life for a lousy story," he finally said.

"Who said it's a lousy story?" I asked, making light of it. "It's a real blockbuster. And you talk about having national interest. I think there's a way to spread the risk a little to take us away from the center of attraction."

"And how's that?"

"Well," I said, "I owe Stan in Washington a shot at a part of this story. If I know him, he'll play up the photo of this Triad warlord with a prominent Democratic Party fund-raiser and use that tie while our story breaks at the same time using more of a local theme. That'll put this on a national level and make it much riskier for them to try anything against us."

My reasoning didn't fool him. "Man, you're really reaching. But I agree that Stan has to be given something for what he's done."

"He'll give the *Digest* mention. Hell, Bill, you may even get invited to 'This Week with Sam and Cokie.'" I was referring to the popular ABC Sunday morning political television talk show.

"I still don't know. I really have a problem with putting you at this much risk, because it's clearly you they'll go after. Let's face it, this isn't a local Boy Scout troupe we're playing with."

"Bill, I've written about the Mafia a dozen times and I've been threatened by them just as many, and I'm still here."

"That's different. The Mafia, as ruthless as they are, play by the rules. They don't go after the press. They know that's off limits. These guys play by a different set of rules, and I believe they have the same philosophy that the late Aristotle Onassis had when he said, 'The only rules are, that there aren't any rules,' or something like that."

I wanted to run the story and told him so. "It's your paper and you have to make the ultimate decision. I'm going to write the story and put it on your desk. What you do with it, is your decision, knowing I want you to print it."

With that, I was finally able to go to the toilet, then to the computer where I started to write the story.

Identity of Mystery Woman Uncovered.

The investigation into the death of Susan Wong-McCloskey continues to have bizarre twists. In the last issue of the *Digest*, we reported that the true identity of the victim was not known, but that she had assumed the identity of the deceased Susan Wong of Great Falls, Montana.

Sources in Hong Kong reveal that

the deceased is Ling Mae, the former mistress of a noted Chinese Triad leader who fled that colony at approximately the same time she assumed the name of Susan Wong. Hong Kong authorities now believe that the Triad leader resides in the Los Angeles area.

These same sources believe that the travel agency operated by the deceased was involved in the smuggling of illegal aliens from China into the United States. Offices of the travel agency, U.S. Tours, were broken into several days ago and all files were taken.

Triads, an Asian equivalent of the Italian Mafia, date back to the 17th century and flourished in Hong Kong during the first half of the 20th century. Their power diminished during a government crackdown in 1956, and they became little more than street gangs. They staged a comeback during the 1980's. Their main criminal activities are extortion, loan sharking, credit card fraud and video piracy.

Some Triad members eventually immigrated to Great Britain where they are considered a "criminal cancer" and are looked upon as a major threat.

DEATH ON THE HILL

In the United States, the FBI began recognizing the problem of Asian organized crime in 1984. In 1987, the Bureau included Asian organized crime within the priorities of its organized crime national strategy.

Initially, the FBI's Asian organized crime program focused on groups believed to have the greatest potential to evolve into organizations which might rival the criminal influence of La Cosa Nostra, more commonly referred to as the Mafia. These included Triads and Tongs.

The FBI believes these groups to be highly organized, well-structured, extremely profitable, and often violent criminal enterprises, posing a serious threat to communities across the United States. The FBI reports that Asian criminal enterprises are becoming increasingly more significant in the United States, moving into criminal activities once thought to be the sole province of the Mafia. With the Asian population in the United States expected to grow to fifteen million by the year 2002, (of which Los Angeles is expected to have 41%), the FBI fears a significant expansion of criminal activity as the Asian mobsters seek to expand their criminal influence.

The Bureau considers Asian criminal enterprises such a threat that their activity aimed at that problem was one of only two FBI-organized crime/drug programs to receive funding in the 1995 budget. It is one of the main reasons the FBI has established an overseas presence.

In writing the article, I leaned heavily on the speech of FBI director Louis Freeh to the 17th Annual International Asian Organized Crime Conference in Boston, Massachusetts in March 1995. It was the same speech that Carleton Yang had told me about during our first visit.

After completing the piece, I read it over. I was satisfied that this should get someone's attention, wondering if the good people residing on the Palos Verdes Peninsula had ever seen numbers like this before. The only danger in an article like this was that it could give the wrong impression, and gloss over the fact that the Asian community, as Director Freeh had said, is truly dedicated to family values and possesses a strong work ethic. Their kids are always at the top of the class when it comes to academics. Their presence at universities has led many people to fear that if students are given admission solely on the basis of grades, UCLA will truly stand for "Us Caucasians Lost Among Asians." That frightens some people. I hoped the piece wouldn't fuel that fire of fear.

Bill was still staring out into space when I handed him my work.

I retreated to my rabbit hutch and called Stan in

Washington. I told him the gist of my story and promised to fax him a copy. He was going to handle the tie between the Triad boss and the Democratic fundraiser on his end. I also called my friends at the *Great Falls, Montana Trib* and gave them the same info and the same promise. They told me that they didn't have anything more on their end yet, but believed the local cops had a list of the names and dates of all the local Chinese that died within a year of the dates the real Susan Wong died. They could probably get a copy of it. I told them that I would find out how old the Triad warlord was and feed it to them to narrow the list down.

Bill popped his head in and told me that he had decided to run the piece. It was just too good to ignore, but I had to promise to be extra careful. He even wanted to hire a private detective to protect me. I respectfully declined.

"Then let's get out a paper," he said, and we went to work doing just that.

It might have been Saturday, but Detective Bilbo tracked us down at Bill's before noon. Bill was still in his blue and yellow spandex, and I was in my usual pair of faded jeans. I hadn't even bothered to put a shirt on yet. At eleven on a Saturday morning, it was still too early to think about getting dressed.

We were sitting in the courtyard, Bill sipping orange juice and me drinking black coffee. One of Bill's neighbors told him we reminded her of the old "Odd Couple" movie with Walter Mathau and Jack Lemmon. I never saw that movie, but remember the television show with Tony Randall and Jack Klugman before he became Quincy. I don't think Bill and I were quite as bad as Felix and Oscar. Bill may be a health nut, but he's not a neat freak. I might like to look like a slob on weekends and enjoy red meat and beer, but I at least throw the sheet over the pillows in the morning, hang up my towel and put my dirty clothes in the clothes hamper.

The topic of our morning's conversation was our article on the murder. We were still congratulating ourselves on the way it had come out. Bill still had some trepidation about it, wondering if it looked like we were being racist and anti-Asian. I'd had the same problem when I was writing the piece but, as I told him then and I was telling him again this morning, "Everything that was said is factual, and most of it was taken directly from either the speech by the Director of the FBI or the U.S. Census Bureau."

That led us to an intense conversation regarding the right to free speech, which, as journalists, we were both adamant about. When the doorbell rang we had both agreed that the political correctness craze was becoming extremely nauseating and, as journalists, we should continue to be sensitive about those issues, though we couldn't ignore the facts because some people are over sensitive.

"Who could that be on a Saturday morning?" Bill remarked, as he went to the intercom. The voice on the other end was Detective Bilbo, asking if he could come in and talk with us.

Joining us on the patio, Bilbo apologized for bothering us on the weekend, then said, "You guys are digging up things that are mighty interesting and I thought we should have a little off-the-record chat."

Since I didn't know what to say, I just sat there, silently

drinking my coffee. I didn't want to abandon Bill but, when push came to shove, it had to be Bill's decision. It was his paper, his liability and, above all, his community. This is exactly what I told him when we excused ourselves and went into the living room, telling the detective that we needed to caucus.

Like all good editors I have ever worked with, Bill accepted the responsibility and told me to follow his lead.

Bill headed back to the table with renewed vigor and took on the offense. I noticed that he remained standing while he talked to Bilbo. "We'll be as candid and open with you as we can," said Bill, "but you know that we're not required to identify our sources, and we won't name names. However, we'll tell you what we can while protecting those sources. Agreed?"

"Agreed," Bilbo replied, looking up at Bill. "I'll do the same, with the understanding that, unless I say differently, what I'm going to tell you is off the record."

"No," Bill said, retaking his seat. "I'd rather not be put in that situation. I'd rather take the position that whatever you tell us is on the record except when you specifically say it's off the record, because we may have already uncovered the same thing from another source and have already made the decision to use it."

I could see by his face that Bilbo didn't really care for this, but he agreed anyway. "What you have come up with makes good reading and I have to admit, has helped us in our investigation. But, except for trying to establish motive, we are looking for the killer of Mrs. McCloskey, which is how we've taken to identifying her. The crime we are trying to solve is still her murder. Triad warlords, as you put it, who are wanted in Hong Kong, but who haven't broken the law here, aren't in our jurisdiction unless someone asks us to detain them for extradition."

"So you shouldn't be upset with us for coming forth with what we have," I interjected.

Bilbo turned his attention to me. "I'm not the least bit upset, but can't speak for my chief when I make that statement. He's upset that it makes us look like we aren't doing our job."

Bill cut in, "Okay. Let me tell you what we have." He went on to tell Bilbo about our contacts in Chinatown without naming names, and how one of them came up with a picture from a Democratic fundraiser, which showed a prominent Democrat with the unidentified man. He was doing a masterful job of telling Bilbo everything without telling him anything that he hadn't already read about in the *Peninsula Digest*.

In return, Bilbo told us that he had sent the fingerprints of the deceased to the FBI lab in Washington, and so far they had drawn a blank. He was surprised when he read in the paper this morning that we had done what the FBI couldn't do, which prompted his decision to come and see us. He dropped the real bombshell when he told us that a motel owner had come forth and told them that a person who looked like the deceased had checked into his motel with a younger woman every week for the past six months.

I asked if they had registered, knowing it would have been an assumed name, but also knowing that handwriting analysis could determine if it was Susan Wong-McCloskey's. He told me that the couple had registered and that the analysis had already been done. It had been determined that the handwriting was not Susan's.

"Sounds like Mrs. McCloskey was a switch hitter," I

replied, "and the other one signed the register."

"That's a possibility," said Bilbo. "But, unless we locate the other person, we'll never know for sure." He went on to tell us that he did have confirmation that the dead woman was not Susan Wong, but he added, "Since she was married, she is, or was, legally, Susan McCloskey." Beyond that, they had been "running into a stonewall" and had nothing. None of the neighbors had heard or seen anything. There was nothing from which they could get a DNA or blood sample. There were no fingerprints and no clothing. They had no forensic evidence.

I sneaked a quick glance at Bill and saw the look of empathy come across his face. I knew he was feeling sorry for Bilbo, but Bill was a newspaperman through and through. I had faith he wouldn't let sympathy stand in the way of a legitimate story.

He didn't disappoint me. He continued to look directly at Bilbo and said, "Just for your information, we're going to continue actively pursuing the Triad and illegal immigration angles. We're not out to solve the murder for you. That doesn't mean we won't cooperate with the police, but we do have a parochial interest in breaking stories before our much larger rivals."

"I admit," Bilbo said, "that the department has a long-standing relationship with the *Breeze* and the *Times* and, except for what I don't make generally known at the station, I can't guarantee nothing won't be leaked."

It was pretty clear that he was a totally frustrated cop who was getting pressured to solve a case that was completely void of clues. He was right that our stories were far off the field of what he was investigating, but he also knew that what we'd come up with had a bearing on his case. In addition, he realized, but couldn't admit, that at this point in time, we had a better chance of getting to the bottom of the case than he did. It was to his advantage to work closer with us than vice-versa.

After Bilbo left, I complimented Bill on the way he handled the situation and thanked him for not saying anything about the detectives from Hong Kong. We then got down to the serious business of making plans for the rest of the weekend.

CHAPTER TEN

With Lucinda working, and Bill not wanting to get involved with anyone of the opposite sex until he had his business under control, our Saturday night turned out to be a movie and dinner in Redondo Beach.

I'm sure that people, including Bill's neighbors, thought we were gay, since I was obviously living there and they didn't see a parade of young females. They didn't, however, know my friend Bill and how focused he could be.

Bill knew his frailties. In that respect, he hadn't changed all that much, for he was a one-woman man. He didn't seek one-night stands. He was the direct opposite of a wrecking ball in search of a building to demolish. Even when he was sowing the wild oats of yesteryear, when Bill fell, he fell hard. To my knowledge he'd never once cheated on a woman he was dating, let alone his former wife. Every relationship he went into, he went into for eternity. Lucinda should have met him instead of me.

Bill knew that when he met another Ms. Right, he would take his eye off the ball and devote too much time to her to the point of worship. In his mind, it was better not to get involved with anyone on the chance that he would fall in love and have to make a choice between a woman and his newspaper.

A corporate executive once told me that the hardest part of his job was balancing his home life with his business life. "Some people can handle it," he had said, "and others like me, can't.

Since Rita had left, I'd felt the best way to balance the two was to give up one of those lives. I never remarried and I was still a reporter. As I pondered this some more, maybe I *was* cheating. Only my mistress wasn't another woman. It was the *Chicago Trib*.

The movie was lousy. It was one of those no plot, special effects extravaganzas. The only acting consisted of the female lead walking with boobs swaying in the wind while tush and fabric were engaged in a struggle for survival. The male star's contribution was an exposed hairy chest, the flexing of silicon biceps, and close ups of twenty-two year old buns. I counted no less than eight chase scenes, all on deserted streets of Los Angeles. That alone made it science fiction.

I was grateful that dinner was another story. I had eaten in some of the best restaurants in the country and this one rated right up there with the best.

Such was our Saturday night out on the town. We were in bed, in separate rooms, before midnight.

I make it a habit to put a pencil and paper on my nightstand so that I can write down things that come to mind when I'm in that zone between consciousness and slumber land. The next morning what my subconscious thought was a great idea usually seemed ridiculous.

Keeping a pad and pencil to write down thoughts in Bill's guest bedroom was a feat unto itself. Bill was a fully functioning bachelor. The furnishings of his guestrooms were similar to the stocking of his refrigerator. As such, they consisted of a bed, and everything else was pure fluff.

Luckily for me, when Bill bought the headboard it had a small nightstand built onto it. The salesperson must have recommended that he purchase a lamp to go on the headboard. Not so lucky for me and my note taking, however. The lamp was lacking an adequate bulb.

I was in that never-never land going over the murder investigation. Bilbo had been right. We had stirred up a lot of ancillary information, but not much on the crime itself. My revelation was that the key to the actual crime might just be with the two detectives from Hong Kong. I jotted down a couple of questions for them: (1) What was the age of the Triad warlord for Great Falls? and (2) Was there a pattern to the warlord's gang murders?

The Hong Kong detectives, Carleton Yang and Sun Fu Yee didn't know about the severed ears. If the gang had that as an M.O., then we would know who was responsible for the killing. As I wrote this down, I jotted down some questions for myself. If the warlord arranged for the killing, why would he want his mistress to die, and why did he allow his mistress to marry an airline captain?

These were the things going through my mind as I turned off the light and rolled over to try and get some sleep. I heard the telephone ring. Bill called out that it was Lucinda. My mind was really heading toward fantasyland as I raced down the stairs barefoot and in my underwear.

My fantasies crumbled as soon as I heard her voice.
"The woman is here in the restaurant," she said.
"What woman?"
"The one we followed when we got run off the road,

dummy," she replied.

"Oh, that woman." The significance of what she was saying began to register. "Is she alone?"

"Yes. What do you want me to do?"

I didn't know what she should do. Yet, I couldn't tell her to do nothing. I had to say something. Luckily my instinct was better than my conscious judgment. "You need to get something that hasn't been touched by several people," I said, "like a clean coffee cup, and preserve it so that it has only her finger prints on it. Then put it in a plastic bag and save it for me."

"Okay, gotta go. Call me tomorrow," she said as she hung up.

It was only then that I saw Bill standing at the entrance to the room. His attire of white Fruit of the Loom briefs was identical to mine. I think mine had a larger bulge in the front than his, but I had just been speaking to Lucinda. I told him about the conversation.

"I hope she doesn't do anything stupid like following the woman when she leaves," said Bill.

"Don't think she will. The little episode of being run off the road squelched her desire to be an ace detective."

"You want a cup of tea or something?" asked Bill. "I don't think I can go back to sleep right now."

"Yeah, I'll join you. Funny thing, when you called me to the phone, I had just jotted down some notes. By the way, do you have a higher watt light bulb? That one's so dim that I feel like young Abe Lincoln trying to read in front of the fire."

Bill handed me a new 75-watt bulb. "Here. Try this." Then he filled a copper kettle with water and put it on the stove.

"Why don't you just put water in cups and microwave them?" I asked.

"Because I don't like using microwaves," Bill answered. "Those waves of radiation don't do you any good. If I had cancer and had to undergo chemotherapy, I'd do it for survival. But given a choice, I'd prefer not to. That's why." He looked at me questioningly. "Am I missing something? What does the microwave have to do with the killing of Susan Wong?"

I threw up my hands. "Nothing. I was just curious."

Screwing up his face in obvious disgust at my diversion into trivia, he went on. "We have to find out more about the Triad boss, like how old he is, his modus operandi and things like that, because he's the key to the puzzle."

I placed the light bulb on the cocktail table hoping that I wouldn't forget it when I went back to my bedroom, then joined him in the kitchen. "I made a note to ask the detectives from Hong Kong those very questions," I informed him. I also told him about my thoughts on the severed ears.

As I was talking, I noticed Bill taking the tea bag out of one mug and placing it in the other. I couldn't let it pass. "Bill, if you're running out of tea bags, I'll pick some up in the morning, but I'd like mine to at least change the color of the water."

He replied sheepishly. "There's no sense in being wasteful. Tea bags are perfectly capable of making two cups of strong tea."

I felt like kicking myself in the rear end all the way to Chicago and back. I had been so hung up on my wonderful favor for him that I never once contributed to household funds. The guy was probably in debt up to his eyeballs from buying the paper, and here I was sponging off of him like a relative rather than a friend.

My next move was totally spontaneous. I put my arm around him. "I'm sorry for being so damn stupid and insensitive, old buddy. That was a dumb thing to say to a person who I've been freeloading off of for a week."

He put his arm around my waist and replied. "Hey, I asked you to come out, and you're really helping me at the paper. Hell, I was just being cheap. I can afford a tea bag."

"Yeah," I said removing my arm. "But the question is, can you afford the tea bag and your payments on the paper?"

He laughed. "Well, now you know my secret. I'm making the payments by stretching the amount of cups I can get out of one tea bag. When I do it right, I've gotten up to three cups of tea per bag. Not bad, huh?"

"Now I'm afraid to ask for sugar."

"That, I have plenty of. But don't ask for Equal. I don't believe in using chemicals."

I took my mug and sat down at the kitchen table. "Seriously, Bill. I know it's none of my business but, are you hurting?"

He sat down at the other end. "You're right, it's none of your business. Yes, it is a stretch to make the payments on the paper and the mortgage here, but it's doable."

I confessed, "I've never owned anything except a car. Of course, there is one thing we both have in common."

"What's that?" he asked.

"Neither one of us can afford pajamas, slippers or bathrobes."

"Hell," he said rising from the table. "Let's get some sleep. Maybe you want to stay up all night, but I have to go riding in a few hours."

"Just be quiet when you leave," I replied, as I did the same, forgetting the light bulb.

I was still sleeping soundly when I heard the phone ringing downstairs. Bill didn't answer it, so the debate was raging in my mind if I should jump out of bed or let the machine get it. The machine won. I did manage to see if I could hear whose voice it was. I recognized the high-pitched sound of the lovely senorita whom I hadn't been seeing enough of lately. From a purely medical perspective, my testosterone level had been getting dangerously high lately, and I needed to do something about it before a massive explosion occurred. The possibility of seeing Lucinda this morning was enough to get me out of bed.

I don't know what I had expected, but the message was simple. "I have what you wanted me to get. I'll be in most of the morning. Give me a call." No love you, miss you or outflows of affection.

I called her back and she answered on the second ring. I could hear the laughter in her voice. "Did I get you out of bed?"

Of course she knew that she had, but I lied anyway. "No, I was out on the courtyard talking to a neighbor." I didn't even know a neighbor.

She got right to the point. "I have a spoon that she used to stir her coffee with. I made sure that no one else's fingerprints could possibly be on it. I took it out of the dishwasher myself and held it in a place she wouldn't and placed it on the table. I saw her use it. Then, when she left, I placed it in a plastic sandwich bag and put it in my purse.

It's still there."

"You're a complete sweetheart. Can I come over and get it this morning?"

"I wish you would. My roommate's gone home to Santa Barbara this weekend, and there's nobody here but me."

I didn't know she had a roommate. I had never seen any signs of one when I had been in her apartment. But I didn't give the spoon or the roommate another thought as I hung up the phone, cleaned up, put on a pair of shorts and polo shirt, and made it down the hill to her open arms, faster than lawyers get to accidents.

Much, much later, Lucinda retrieved her purse from the table in her living room and brought it back to the bed. Just as she said, the spoon was encased within a sandwich baggy, which she gave to me. When she took out the spoon, a piece of paper came out with it, which she opened and handed to me. "I forgot I even had this. It's the address from the night we were almost killed."

At that moment I don't know what had me more excited, the thought of more erotica in Redondo with Lucinda, knowing the address, or the spoon with fingerprints. Since it was Sunday, there was nothing I could do about the fingerprints. I could drive by the house later, so my short-term priorities came back into focus.

When I got back home, Bill was ready to leave. He had been invited to dinner at the home of a married friend and apologized profusely about leaving me alone. I assured him that I was very happy to spend the night watching an old movie on AMC. This seemed to satisfy him, since he knew I was an old movie freak. I didn't bother to tell him about the sudden emergence of the address, but I showed him the spoon. He volunteered to take it to the security service for fingerprinting the next day.

I retrieved the light bulb and went upstairs to take a shower before settling down for a night with William Powell as "The Thin Man." I was in bed asleep before Bill got back home. In fact, I didn't even hear him come in. It's great how a day of physical exercise can make a person sleep well at night.

The next day I arrived at the paper before Bill returned from the security service. It was part of my new resolve to help Bill as much as I could. There was a message for me to call Sun Fu Yee, which I did.

The photographer had immediately recognized the picture. He had taken one right after that with another man in the background, who had gotten very upset. The man had even offered to purchase the film from the camera. The photographer had declined, but had told the man that if he objected that much, that picture wouldn't be developed. The man had been satisfied and had handed the photographer a hundred-dollar bill.

The photographer had kept his promise, but the image was still on the role of negatives. If it had been anyone but Sidney Lu he wouldn't have made a print. Sidney had taken the print without telling him anything else. The next time he heard about it was from the goons that had beat him up. They had been looking for the negatives and any prints he had made.

What Yee said cleared up only one point that had been bothering me, which was why Lu had sent us a picture without the woman who had been murdered in it? However, I still didn't understand how the Triad warlord found out that Sidney had gotten the picture. I asked Yee, but he was in the dark, too. Sidney must have talked to someone about it. I had to leave it at that.

Just as I hung up with Yee, Bilbo called. He congratulated me on my sources. He had just heard from the FBI that they didn't have any matches to Susan Wong-McCloskey's prints. I didn't think they would have, but I didn't tell him that. The poor guy was having enough problems going through standard police investigative procedure without my gloating. He admitted that the official investigation was going nowhere. I told him that I'd let him know if my sources turned up anything else.

The next item on my agenda was a phone call to Carleton Yang. He took my call immediately. I asked him to find out the approximate age of the Triad warlord.

"He was fifty-eight his last birthday," Yang quickly replied. "April 22."

He didn't even ask me why I needed the information. I guess he took the attitude that, if I wanted him to know, I would have told him. Nice trait to have, but he'd make a terrible newspaper person. I thanked him and told him that I would be in touch.

Bill returned and we talked in his office. I told him how I intended to proceed with our investigation.

"Sounds good to me," he replied, pushing the phone over to me. "Why don't you just call Great Falls from here. I think they're only an hour earlier than we are."

I did and they were. When I told them the age of the Triad warlord they said that a copy of the same list the Great Falls Police Department had sent to the Palos Verdes Police Department was in the mail.

After telling them the essence of the last story we had

run, they asked if I would fax them the entire piece. The saga had really connected with their readers so they wanted us to fax every story that we ran, including photographs.

"See, Bill. The *Peninsula Digest* is already famous in Great Falls, Montana." I said this jokingly.

"Wonderful," replied Bill. "But I don't think I'll take all the subscription revenue to the bank just yet."

It wasn't even noon and I felt like I had done a day's work already. I sat at my desk and contemplated what to do next. I took the address on Via Coronel out of my pocket and decided to take a little drive.

After retrieving the beast of a Toyota, I headed westward on Hawthorne Boulevard toward the ocean. As usual, the sun had come out, there was virtually no wind, and the temperature was in the high seventies. Nothing unusual, just your typical Palos Verdes day.

I followed Hawthorne Boulevard past the Granvia Altimira turnoff, past the sign leading to the Los Verdes Golf Course and over the next hill where I descended into a panoramic seascape. In the middle of the seascape, just before it reached the end of the canvas, I turned right on Palos Verdes Drive toward Lunada Bay.

I followed the same route Lucinda and I had followed after leaving the Admiral Risty. I instinctively ducked when I came to the house where I had gone through the fence (which already had been replaced) and continued up the hill until I came to the right address. How different it looked in the daylight. The house was on my left and a ravine on my right. There was no place to turn off the road to get a better look.

After my second drive-by, I hadn't learned anything more than I'd learned from the first drive-by. Short of scaling the wall, this reconnaissance was a failure, so I decided to return to the paper and implement plan "B."

By the time I returned, the mail had arrived, including the package from Great Falls that I hoped would contain another piece to our puzzle.

The list contained eighty-seven names. Until the past week, if someone had told me that there were eighty-seven Asians in Great Falls, Montana I would have called them a liar. When I narrowed it to males between the ages of fifty-five and sixty-two, only thirteen names were left.

I set off for the County Recorder's Office. Less than forty-five minutes later, thanks to a very helpful clerk, I had found another missing piece of the puzzle.

When I'd awakened that morning, I'd started hacking a little bit. By the time I got to the Recorder's Office I was on a full-blown coughing jag. Now, as any wife will tell you, it's a really pathetic situation when a man is coming down with a cold. There are no limits to his search for sympathy. I was no exception.

The clerk in the Recorder's Office made the mistake of looking at me with a motherly expression and saying, "Poor baby, you seem to be coming down with a cold."

That was all I needed. I sensed immediately that in my hour of need, providence had delivered me into the hands of a caring person. I would be a disgrace to my gender if I didn't milk this kind lady for all the empathy she was capable of emitting.

As I leaned on the counter while she was looking up information for me, my coughing became harsher and more frequent. By the time she returned to the counter, I was having a spasm. I didn't intentionally bring this on. I didn't have to. It happens by itself if you cough long and deep enough. The lungs can sense when they're needed to put on an Emmy caliber performance. The tickle in the throat sends the message that a mother figure has been sighted. They know they must quickly rise to the next level to exploit the opportunity. If they have done their jobs correctly, the male's sympathy invoking hormone is immediately activated. The chest starts to hurt, triggering a natural reaction to lean forward, clutching it with one hand while the other reaches out desperately seeking help. It would be a cruel woman indeed who could resist such a passionate and desperate plea.

After a cup of water, a reassuring back rub, and an admonishment to go right home and rest, I was on my way back to the Peninsula. Her advice made more sense the closer I got. I was starting to feel like hell. My eyes were feeling droopy, my coughing was getting worse and I had started to sweat. Colds engulf me.

The next morning my gut was hurting from the coughing, and my eyes felt like birds had nested on them all night.

I couldn't understand how I'd caught a cold in Southern California. If I hadn't felt so miserable, I would have been really ticked off.

CHAPTER ELEVEN

After two days of hell, I arose and, once again, took my place among the living. I wasn't completely healed, but I was mobile enough to function out of bed.

Bill's anti-cold formula consisting of Vitamins A, C, E and a multiple as well as garlic pills, aspirin, and a zinc lozenge for my cough made the difference. He also gave me his trusty Arrowhead bottled water, commanding that I empty one such bottle every day.

It was on wobbly legs, but I made it down to the living room to return the telephone calls that had been piling up. The first one I answered was from Carleton Yang. As I dialed the number, I wondered what information he had for me. Yang wasn't the type of person to call just to make small talk. I also didn't figure that Teng and Chen, the Hong Kong detectives, were languishing around in a LA hotel room at the pleasure of the Chinese Government.

I was right. Yang gave me a local number to call. The two detectives had made contact with the local Chinese community leaders and wanted to talk to me. The more I dealt with them, the more I learned about the way the Chinese conducted themselves with occidentals. Rather than telephoning me themselves, they were much more formal about our relationship and preferred to make contact through Carleton Yang until they and I felt comfortable with a more direct association. In his own way, Yang urged me to contact them as quickly as possible. I assured him that my next call would be to them.

I lied. My next call was to Lucinda. She was concerned about my well being. When she hadn't heard from me, she had called, and Bill had told her that I was sick in bed and shouldn't be disturbed. Just hearing her voice made me squirm on the couch. There's something in my chemistry that makes me feel sexy when I have a cold. A lot of good it does me. We did the next best thing— indulging in phone sex until we agreed that the only thing we accomplished was frustrating each other.

Her other agenda was to query me on the murder investigation. It was the first time she had asked about it directly. All the other times it came up as pillow talk, after we had made love. Having been run off the road the night we had gone to the Admiral Risty, it seemed only natural she would have an interest.

After putting a zinc lozenge under my tongue, I returned to the couch and dialed the number that Yang had given me.

The voice of a young lady answered. "Tse residence, may I help you please?" She repeated it in Chinese before I could reply.

I was finally able to identify myself and asked for Mr. Teng or Mr. Chen.

It was Chen who responded. "I hope you are feeling better, Jeremy. I do appreciate you calling. Did you find the information regarding the age of the Triad leader helpful?

"Yes, I did. Thank you. In fact, I believe I now have information that will identify the name the warlord is presently using."

"Now, Jeremy," the detective cautioned, "we should not divulge such information over the phone. If you are well enough, I will arrange for a car to take you to where I am now staying."

I had to smile to myself at his reaction. We tend to forget how secure an ordinary telephone call is when it is placed over the wires in the United States, as opposed to countries less adamant about human rights. I agreed to the arrangement and gave him Bill's address. He said the car would be there in less than an hour.

Before going up to dress, I called Bill at the paper to let him know what was going on. He cautioned me to be careful. I felt so rejuvenated that I took the steps two at a time. There's nothing like mental stimulation to make a person forget he's one step away from hospitalization.

Trying to figure out what to wear was my next obstacle. While I had managed to keep up with my laundry, my dry cleaning suffered. Besides jeans and shorts, I had only brought two pairs of slacks that could remotely be considered good enough for business purposes. I hadn't anticipated that I would be spending time on assignment. A pair of tan pants hanging in the closet weren't wrinkled too badly. Now all I needed was a shirt that didn't look like it was a Salvation Army reject. Then I'd be in business. I lucked out. One of my shirts was found to be presentable. A quick shower later, and I was standing in front of the building awaiting my ride.

There was nothing understated about the black Lincoln Town Car that pulled up in front of me. Detective Chen beckoned me to enter the vehicle.

In the back seat, Chen was alone. A driver and a sober looking younger Asian man dressed like the Blues Brothers, with blue suit, white shirt, and red tie occupied the front. Both the driver and the man riding shotgun were identically dressed.

During our first meeting in Carleton Yang's office, Chen had been extremely quiet. Today he was extremely talkative about everything except what we were supposedly meeting for. I found out how much he loved the California weather and that he was a Western movie buff.

By the time we pulled onto the now familiar Palos Verdes Drive toward Lunada Bay, I knew how many bad guys Audie Murphy had gunned down in every movie he'd made. When we made the turn onto Via Coronel, he had exhausted Audie Murphy Westerns and had launched into the same analysis of Jimmy Stewart's work.

I was only half listening because I was trying to see exactly where we were going. The first landmark was the infamous fence on the curve at the bottom of the street.

The next milestone was the mansion I had been casing before my bout of illness. We went past that home, and two more before we pulled up to a house not quite as large and pretentious, but just as imposing.

I looked out the back window as we went up the circular driveway, and noted that we were directly opposite the other mansion, only at a higher elevation. The detectives from Hong Kong were either the greatest planners in the world or the luckiest, for they had a perfect vantage point from which to case the place.

Somehow I didn't think this was all coincidence. The

illness of the past couple of days was forgotten by the time the car stopped at a side entrance.

Standing in the open doorway was a smiling Detective Teng. I noticed that they had an even greater wardrobe problem than I did, for they were in the same clothes they had worn at our first meeting. Mr. Teng, like Mr. Chen, seemed to be in good spirits.

"It's nice of you to come," Mr. Teng said as he held out his hand in greeting. "I understand that you have not been well."

"I'm honored to be invited," I replied with as much humility in my voice as I could conjure up.

"Please," he said with a sweeping arm gesture as he moved away from the doorway to leave room for me to pass. "Our host would like to meet with you."

Mr. Chen had already entered the home and was waiting for me as I entered a long hallway. The first thing I noticed was the hardwood flooring polished to such a high brilliance that you could see your reflection. We passed several closed doors before we came to a "T" at the end. My escorts turned left to a foyer from the front entrance. On either side of the marble entry were two steps leading down into separate rooms, both covered with identical deep pile, pale blue carpeting.

A quick glance at both rooms revealed a distinctly Western motif. I could be walking into any corporate tycoon's living and music rooms in any large city in the United States. The furnishings could have come right out of the latest issue of "Architectural Digest." The place had the distinct odor of money... lots of it. It made Bill's place look like a dump, and mine back in Chicago look like something the dump refused. The wooden pieces, such as

155

cocktail table, lamp tables and library table, were made of solid walnut, not veneer. I know, because my second best subject back in high school was shop, and our teacher gave us a quiz every week on the identification of fine and exotic woods. It's something that stayed with me all these years.

Standing at the far end of the room near a large freestanding globe was a Chinese man, probably in his late seventies. Except for his unmistakably Asian facial features, if you saw him from behind, he could have passed for a European or American. He stood at least six feet one or two with an athletic frame, clothed in a stylish Italian-cut business suit. When he walked toward me holding out his hand, I also saw a pinkie ring.

He made his own introduction. "I am George Tse," he said with a tone of someone with authority. "I am very happy to meet such a noted journalist."

Not many people have ever referred to me as "noted" before.

Tse continued. "I have enjoyed your articles on the incident involving the unfortunate Mrs. McCloskey, but one should not be surprised from a person who so brilliantly exposed the atrocious behavior of members of the U.S. Congress. Please have a seat." He pointed me to an oversized white satin Bergere chair. "Would you like a drink?"

I didn't bother to hide my smile. "I see you've done your homework on me." It wasn't the first time I had been exposed to people who roamed the rarefied air of power. The tactic he had just used on me was one of the things a good interviewer learns within the first six months on the job. Never go into an interview without knowing everything you can about the person being interviewed, and then let him know you know. It wouldn't have taken much digging to find out about the incident he was referring to. It had made all the wire services. Still, he had gotten his point across. He knew much more about me than I knew about him, and he had politely let me know just that.

I declined his offer of a drink, as I settled back into the chair.

I employed a tactic of my own by silently just sitting there. The meeting was on their nickel. Not surprisingly, my host assumed command and dispensed with further pleasantries.

"It is our wish that you treat this meeting as 'off the record' until we agree what should be public knowledge. If you can't agree to that, all we can do is thank you for the cooperation you have given us so far and we will see that you get back to your quarters."

I felt like I was being lectured, but I held my emotions in check, and agreed to his demands, except to say that I reserved the right to further negotiation on what could be printed after the meeting was concluded. He looked over at the two detectives who nodded their heads in agreement before he concurred.

"I think first you should understand my role," Tse said as he sat down. "I understand you know the roles of Mr. Chen and Mr. Teng."

I followed his gaze over to the detectives and acknowledged as much.

"Mr. Chen and Mr. Teng were sent to see me by our mutual friend, Mr. Carleton Yang." Tse paused to sip his brandy and, then stood up and walked over to an oil painting of three Chinese men. The oldest in the painting was sitting in a chair flanked on either side by a middle-aged man and one in his mid-twenties. Pointing to the eldest, Tse said with discernible pride, "My grandfather came to this country as a young boy. He worked in a grocery store until he saved enough money to open his own store. Being an ambitious man, he soon opened another store, then another until he had a chain of five local markets. He was not yet 30. He married my grandmother in an arranged marriage, which was the custom at that time in the Chinese community, and started a family. After the birth of his second son, he purchased one of the wholesalers that supplied his stores.

"By the time the last of his five sons was born, he was the largest wholesale supplier of goods to the community. He was still only in his mid-forties. He was determined that each of his sons would benefit from his good fortune and hard work. He made all of them get a college education, something that he didn't have."

He turned back to the painting and pointed at the middle-aged man. "My father was the oldest son and was fortunate to inherit his father's aggressive business acumen. As my grandfather got older, he turned over most of the day-to-day operations to my father. Two brothers entered the business as well, while two others chose engineering careers."

His eyes looked squarely into mine. "I hope I am not boring you, but I believe that what I am telling you will give you a greater understanding of the Chinese heritage in this area. This should help you as you continue your excellent coverage of this incident. I must also be truthful that we are fearful that what is happening may have negative repercussions, due to fear that we are, as some people have suggested, taking over California. I, too, see the numbers and know what they mean."

I noticed his voice became louder and he began speaking more rapidly. "To digress a little, soon the Asian communities in this State will elect one of their own to high political office, either as Governor or United States Senator. That will be inevitable. At this point, many do not vote. Just as many Hispanics stay home on election day. But one day, when they have their own candidate, they will turn out and vote as a block, and then they will win.

"Again, I apologize for digressing. My father and his brothers continued to expand the business, as I have, since I took over from him, with the help of my two brothers and several cousins. We have built our companies to the point where we have virtually a one hundred percent monopoly in the wholesale grocery and restaurant supply business for the Chinese community in the South Bay. We also have a considerable presence in Orange County and parts of the central city." He returned to his seat.

I hadn't moved a muscle since he started his discourse.

Though now seated, Tse wasn't yet finished. "We have heard over the past three or four years that many of the smaller retailers we service have been approached and are paying protection monies to local tongs. There have been sporadic attempts at this in the past but we have managed to keep it invisible, so to speak, by handling it in our own way."

I had a pretty good idea of what he meant, but held my tongue.

"However," Tse said, "the activity has been getting

much more aggressive and better organized, leading us to believe that a Triad leader has emerged. We have you to thank for securing the picture that made it possible to identify who that leader is, which is why we are here now."

Though I had just been the recipient of a very well constructed sales job, the ball had just been thrown back in my court. Even so, I had no illusions that my relationship was only on a "need to know" basis. For Mr. Tse, at least, I think the need consisted of me tempering future articles so as not to rock the boat and inflame an apathetic Caucasian public still content to believe they would always run the place.

I didn't believe Tse's agenda was the same as that of the two detectives, except for getting rid of the Triad warlord. I didn't want to be rude to my host, but I thought a quid pro quo might be in order.

"From your explanation," I said, "you are saying that you have a Chinese community within the South Bay, not that you are Chinese living within the South Bay community. There is a difference. Let me ask you. Are you a Chinese in the local Chamber of Commerce, or do you belong to a Chinese Chamber of Commerce?"

His smile told me that we understood one another. "I think you know the answer to that. I belong to both. I bridge a gap between the two. One of my sons is married to an occidental and doesn't even speak Chinese. As you see from the surroundings, I leave most of my ethnicity at my office, which is one hundred percent Chinese decor. We speak only English in this house, but speak only Chinese in the work environment. Since we are being candid with one another, the bulk of the Chinese community in this area does not embrace Western culture, but is most comfortable in keeping the old ways. From a business standpoint, this is to my advantage. As long as I treat my customers fairly, and bargain honorably with them, I will get their business because they wish to deal with us rather than occidentals. It is no different than the Irish in Boston, the Italians in New York, and the Polish in Chicago."

He had a point, except that the Irish in Boston eventually married the Italians in New York and the Polish in Chicago married the Lithuanians and they branched out from there, but I wasn't invited here for a discourse on the evolution of ethnicity in America. We understood one another and that was all that mattered.

"Touché," I said. "Now I think we should get on with our common problem. Mr. Triad Warlord, as I call him."

Up to this point the two detectives had remained sitting with a bored look on their faces. It was Mr. Teng who spoke. "You mentioned on the telephone that you had some information for us regarding the identity of this man."

I handed him the paper that was folded in my back pocket and said, "After you gave me the age of the person, I sent it to Montana, where we know the woman who was killed got her identity, on the off chance that he might have gone to that same community. The thirteen names you see highlighted are aliases that could be used by your Triad Godfather. If I could access the Social Security Administration, which I can't, it would be simple to find out if any of those names are currently being used. I suppose we could also find out from the California Department of Motor Vehicles if someone with that name has a valid driver's license. That would involve the local police, however, and I don't want them involved just yet."

Mr. Tse asked Detective Teng if he could see the list, which he studied for sometime.

"Unfortunately," said Tse, "most of these names are quite common to run a driver's license check and I don't recognize any of them."

"I might be able to make the search easier." I told them about following the woman who had dinner with McCloskey and being run off the road afterwards. All three followed me to the window. "The person we want may be right in that house over there."

With the four of us clustered around the window, Teng asked Tse in English if he knew who lived there. Tse told him he had never met, or seen, the people. He had assumed there was a large family in the house, which wasn't unusual. Most recent immigrants from Hong Kong and Taiwan brought relatives with them, and he had noticed many cars coming and going. Chen asked about how we could find out.

Tse said he would make some discreet inquires and would eventually find out. When I asked how, he shrugged and said, "If they send their shirts to the laundry or their dry cleaning out, if they order any supplies or have a gardener, I will get names and descriptions. Just leave it to me."

I didn't doubt him for a minute.

We sat back down and Chen addressed me directly. "I must explain that Mr. Teng and I are guests of Mr. Tse in this house, so while Mr. Tse makes his inquires we will be watching the house over there, and observe the movements of the people. It would seem that the distance is not so great that a camera with a high-powered lens should provide us with good pictures which we can send to Hong Kong. Our colleagues there will be able to tell us if they are known criminals. I must ask that for now you do not print anything about what was said here today, and that the local authorities do not know what we are doing. Is that agreed?"

I nodded my head, then added, "As long as I am kept informed and a part of what you are doing, I have no intention of harming your investigation."

"Thank you," Chen replied. "Mr. Yang said that you were an honorable man and would stay by your word."

"Speaking of Mr. Yang," I asked no one in particular, "may I ask what his interest is in this matter?"

As I expected, it was Mr. Tse who spoke. He had been sitting with his hands folded across his lap in a passive manner. When he answered my question, the hands came off the lap as he straightened his back in the chair. "Mr. Yang is a respected man in the Los Angeles Chinese community." I noticed he made a distinction between South Bay and Los Angeles, meaning, I surmised, that Yang's influence was much more encompassing. "We belong to several of the same organizations."

"Is one of them fundraising for the Democratic Party?" I asked.

Tse gave me another one of those all-knowing smiles. "On occasion Mr. Yang and I have helped our political party with monetary assistance."

Although Tse had gotten up from his seat to conclude the meeting, I continued to probe. "Were you by any chance at the fund-raiser where the picture that eventually opened this whole Triad affair was taken? And was Mr. Yang at that same affair?"

Tse held his hand out to shake mine. "We will discuss that at another time, if you don't mind. I'm sorry, but I must go. My driver will take you back to your home. We will be in touch with you. In the meantime, please feel free to call if you have any questions."

I know when I've been dismissed, so I dutifully followed Teng and Chen back through the house to the same black Lincoln with the same driver, only this time minus the guy riding shotgun. I guess they concluded that I was no longer a threat to anyone. Before getting into the car, I told Teng that I would like him and Chen to have dinner with Bill and me, and would call them to arrange a time. They both shook their heads affirmatively and thanked me for the invitation.

A few minutes later I was back at Bill's having a relapse.

CHAPTER TWELVE

It was Wednesday, two days after my visit to Tse's home, before I felt well enough to make any appointments. I had been well during the meeting last Monday, only to come back and collapse. Kneeling on the bathroom floor with my face thrust into the commode, I had upchucked the contents of my stomach. Memories of my early days of trying to drink Chicago dry emerged out of my subconscious. Thanks, but no thanks. Those were the memories I could do without.

When I surfaced and became conscious of what day it was, I realized that I had missed the deadline to contribute a story for Bill's paper. I hadn't had much to contribute anyhow. Being an old hand at the game, Bill would have done a great job regurgitating the entire episode and quoting Detective Bilbo that the police department hadn't turned up any significant leads. This would keep the public interested. It was standard don't-let-the-public-forget-about-it, but-there's-nothing-to write-about fare.

I had awakened determined to get things back on track. Sometimes you just can't let the stories come to you, you have to go to them. I have seen too many good stories die for lack of momentum, and I wasn't about to let this happen to something so important to Bill. The *Daily*

Breeze and *LA Times* were already chasing more topical news events, which is what a public conditioned to twenty-second sound bites responds to. As one of my favorite editors on a rival paper once said, "The public has the attention span of a gnat, so hit them hard and often within that limited window of opportunity."

I figured our window was closing, and we had at most another week to milk it. The Anglo people on the Palos Verdes Peninsula, who would continue to dominate the demographics at least for the next few years, didn't exactly harbor a deep emotional kinship with the departed Susan Wong-McCloskey.

Bill was already at the paper when I awakened, so I called him there to let him know my plans for the day. I told him that, although I felt pretty good and I was once again among the living, I intended to do as much as I could from the house rather than infect his staff. He appreciated my concern. I asked if he would be amenable to having dinner with the two Chinese detectives. He agreed that we should keep that association on the front burner since it was the best thing we had in terms of the case.

When I placed the call, Mr. Teng came on the line. I reminded him about the invitation and asked if this evening was convenient. "One moment please," was the response.

During the silence, I contemplated what I was going to say if they asked where we could meet. I had just made an executive decision when Mr. Chen came back on the line. I told them I would pick them up at Mr. Tse's residence at seven that evening.

I didn't have the faintest idea where to take them but, since Chen was a rabid Western fanatic, a steakhouse seemed like a good idea. But Bill didn't eat red meat, so we needed to go some place where Chen could eat steak and Bill could eat fish. I threw my arms up in frustration and yelled at the potted plant standing in the far corner. "I suppose Teng's a vegetarian. That'd make it complete. Why does it have to be so complicated just to find a place to eat?" Hell, I thought. Bill's the boss around here. I'll do what every red blooded male does when he doesn't know what to do. I'll buck the decision upstairs. I jerked the phone off of the cocktail table and called Bill. It was his problem now.

I didn't know why I'd gotten so upset over so little. It may have been because I still wasn't feeling like myself, or because this damned case wasn't coming to closure fast enough. In my mind, I had a pretty good idea of who the principal players were and where it was headed, but I was having a tough time putting all the pieces in their proper places.

The puzzle was gradually coming together, but not to the extent that I could write about it without subjecting my friend Bill to a gigantic libel suit. There were just a few more manipulations that I had to engineer before I could get out the laptop and draft my epistle. In the meantime, I had to put all my facts and assumptions down in writing. But first, it was time to take a shower. I was starting to stink. All morning I'd been lounging on Bill's couch in the same underwear that I had put on Monday morning. My habit of wearing underwear to bed used to drive Rita crazy. She'd always slept in the buff.

The PV police and the county sheriff's department were looking at the murder as one tree, while the Hong Kong detectives were looking at the Triad warlord as another tree. We were the only people looking at it as one with several branches. In fact, the murder of Sidney was being looked at as a third tree by the LAPD. I knew simply from watching the television news that there were other people looking at the fund raising situation as yet another tree. This could be right since, other than the photograph of people attending a common function, there was nothing to tie it in with the murder or the Triad warlord. The guy could just have been invited to a party. Most fund raising affairs I'd ever covered had only one thing as the criterion for an invitation—the ability to write a check that won't bounce.

I became convinced that the key to solving the case rested with the Chinese detectives. Early in the case, I'd thought that we had a better chance to solve the mystery than the police did. Nothing so far had changed the situation. Tonight's dinner with the detectives could be crucial to facilitating closure.

Reluctantly, I turned off the shower, dried myself and confronted my next problem—what to wear. Poking my head out of the window, that decision turned into a no brainer. It was shorts weather. Now all I had to do was find a clean pair. Rummaging through my suitcase I found a pair of green K-Mart specials with coordinating top. I made a mental note to do some laundry right after I finished my phone calls.

I dressed and headed back down the stairs for a cup of decaffeinated tea and an English Muffin without butter. Disgusting, but I was actually getting used to living this way.

Unlike Bill, I put a cup of water in the microwave and three minutes later was sipping a cup of hot tea. Basking in my inventiveness, I returned to the couch and got down to business.

My first call was to Sun Fu Yee, whom I hadn't talked to in awhile. Yee wasn't home so I left a message on his answering machine that I'd called with nothing in particular, but just to touch base.

My next call to Stan in Washington was equally frustrating. Another answering machine on which I left the same message. Disgusted, I hung up and called Bill again. I didn't get voice mail this time, but the results were the same ... Bill was out of the office. The receptionist promised that Bill would call me when he walked in. I asked her if Bill had made reservations for dinner that night. She told me he hadn't, but she had. We were set for the Papadakis Taverna in San Pedro at seven thirty.

Just as she was about to give me her recommendation on what to order at Papadakis, she announced that Bill had just returned.

No sooner had she spoken the words and Bill was on the phone. "I have your fingerprints," he told me.

"What do you need my fingerprints for?" I replied. "You can't convict a person for wanting to kill his ex-wife."

That got a laugh out of him. Mentioning the thought of killing an ex-wife is always good for a laugh when you're talking to a divorced man. "Pick a jury of men and you'd never get convicted," he said. "But that's not what I meant. I forgot who I was dealing with. I have the fingerprints from the spoon that your concubine gave you."

"Very funny," I said, "being a concubine refers to cohabitation of persons not legally married. Which means it doesn't apply to Lucinda and me."

"Anyway. I'll bring them home with me."

"Good," I replied. "I want to give them to our guests tonight to send to Hong Kong. Maybe it'll help us to get this thing wrapped up. After all, we don't have to convince twelve peers beyond a shadow of a doubt."

"We don't want to go to court for libel either. Hey, I'll be home by six, and I am looking forward to meeting the Chinese detectives.

I felt good when I put the phone back down. Bill was a good newspaperman. Having him at the dinner tonight was going to be fun and beneficial. We were getting close to the kill, and I was dangerous when I smelled blood. My natural hip shooting tendency rose to the surface and I tended to go right for the jugular under those circumstances. It wouldn't hurt at all to have a cool hand like Bill around.

There was nothing for me to do but wait. Lucinda was visiting her sister in Orange County. I decided to take advantage of the Southern California weather while I still had the chance, and take a walk along the water.

Since I had walked along the Esplanade in Torrance and Redondo, I decided to walk now along the cliffs overlooking the ocean near Lunada Bay. Bill had driven me by the place pointing out the cliff dwellings of several of the area's well-known citizens. Knowing my weakness for movies, he also pointed out the cliff where they filmed the sports car going over the cliff in "Resurrection."

Walking along the cliffs turned out to be a good idea. There was a gently cooling ocean breeze that hardly ruffled the leaves on the gigantic palms. Off in the distance, freighters and container vessels steamed toward the distant Pacific Rim countries from the Port of Los Angeles, which is actually located in San Pedro.

Stopping to watch the ships inching their way out of the bay, gave my imagination a field day. I had a difficult time deciding which ship I was on. Was it the first one about to disappear over the horizon bound for far off Casablanca where Humphrey Bogart was lighting another cigarette while still pining for Ingrid Bergman? Or was it the second one, still visible to the naked eye, on its way to Tahiti where I would meet up with Paul Gauguin and paint beside him as he transformed the island's beautiful women into international starlets? Why have to make a choice? Through the magic of a fertile imagination, I would be on both.

It took me a little over an hour to walk from where I had parked my car at the north end of Paseo del Mar to a natural stopping point where the street curved away from the ocean and back again. I had met only a couple of other cliff wanderers during my entire walk, a rarity in heavily congested Southern California. No wonder the local population resented sharing their idyllic setting with the newcomers. I remember Bill saying when I first arrived, that the Palos Verdes Peninsula is the best-kept secret in Los Angeles. Beverly Hills is gauche elegance while Palos Verdes is country grace.

Returning to the couch, I dialed Stan's number. He answered immediately. "Where's that big story?"

I brought him up to date on what was happening, making a point to tell him that, when it came to his interest—Asian contributions to the Democratic National Committee—I had nothing. "However, Stan. I'm at a point here where we're going to have closure pretty quick, although the local police don't know it yet. But I have to know more about Sun Fu Yee. I have a plan in mind to force the issue, but I don't know enough about him to know where to place him in the final scenario."

"I'll call you back on a hard line in about fifteen minutes, not more."

I had only taken two more gulps of my water before Stan called back. "Can't trust the security of the cell phone, particularly in this town." He quickly got to the point of the call. "To put it in simple terms, Yee is with the Bureau, as in FBI, assigned to the Los Angeles area as part of Freeh's fight against Asian Organized Crime. He's also actively engaged in the Justice Department's investigation of illegal campaign contributions. Yee has been a friend for some time, and when you called, and particularly after the picture showing the very person Yee has been going after, he became interested.

"Let's put it this way. If you put it to him as a hypothetical situation beforehand, he'll be square with you and find a way to let you know that without telling you."

Like most reporters, I've been down that route before, so I knew exactly what Stan was telling me. While I had him in a talkative mood, I thought I'd push it some more. "Now let's go to Carleton Yang and Sidney Lu. Particularly Yang, since he's alive and has been really helpful, as well as trusting."

His description of Yang's character fit my take on him to a tee. "Yang's one of those people you don't run into often. A real gentleman who is also very cognizant of the problem his people will be facing, as they become more numerous here in the States. In fact, Yang would like to see the immigration tide slow down, particularly in Southern California. He's very worried that the rapid flow from Hong Kong and Taiwan, as well as the Philippines, is going to cause tensions that could be avoided if immigration happened at a more gradual pace.

"He's also concerned that his people will be equated with the illegals from Mexico and Central America by most of the Anglo population. I guess you can say he has the same attitude that the European immigrants had in the early 1900's—learn English as quickly as possible and integrate into society while maintaining your heritage."

"So, how'd you meet up with him?" I inquired. "And Sidney Lu?"

"Sidney and I met at that same symposium, quite independently from Yang. Sidney was attending as part of his Community Relations job for the City of Los Angeles. I turned Sun Fu Yee onto him."

"That's interesting," I said. "Yee admitted to knowing Carleton Yang, and, in fact, volunteered it, but didn't mention he knew Sidney Lu."

"Don't forget he's still a cop, even if it is with the Bureau. And you're a newspaper man. He's not going to tell you everything, just as you aren't going to tell him everything. Anyway, I hope I've been helpful, but I've gotta go. Keep me posted."

With nothing better to do, I took a nap on the patio's chaise lounge. I was still sprawled out on it when Bill came home from the paper. He'd thought at first that we were having an earthquake, but the closer he came to the place, the more he recognized the distinctive flutter when I exhaled at the end of my snore. I didn't doubt it. My throat tasted like someone had just dumped an ashtray in it, and I don't smoke. It was so bad that I think he saved my life when he tossed another bottle of water to me as I was trying to disengage my body from the seat cushions.

After I regained my composure, I asked about the restaurant. "The place we're going to eat tonight is Papadakis Taverna. Is it Greek?"

Bill responded with a puzzled look on his face, "I don't know, I've never been there."

It was my turn to look puzzled "Pardon me for being so dense, but if you've never been there, how did you choose the place?"

"I didn't. I told Michelle, our receptionist, that we were taking a couple of people out to dinner tonight and to make us a reservation at one of her favorite restaurants. She's single, really pretty, and wears classy clothes. Guys pick her up in Beemer's, so I figured she goes out to a lot of good places. Why?"

"Well, I thought it odd that we'd take a couple of Chinese men to a Greek restaurant, that's all?"

"Greek's as good as anything. No sense taking them to a Chinese place, they get plenty of that at home, right?"

"What the hell," I replied. "If they don't like it, that's their problem. All I care about is that we have a place we can talk. I figured it's time to force the issue and get something going."

That got Bill's attention. He sighed with relief when I told him what I had in mind. "The way you put it at first, I thought it was going to be something really radical."

Driving to the Tse house, I showed Bill the mansion I was sure housed the Triad warlord. Bill thought it looked like an impregnable fortress. I told him all the places on this part of the hill looked like they could withstand a siege from the barbarians.

When we arrived at Tse's, we pulled up to the front

door. Before we could get out of the car the door opened and the two detectives emerged smiling. I noticed that they both had different suits on than when I had seen them on the last two occasions. I introduced Bill as the Publisher of the *Peninsula Digest.*

They didn't ask, and I didn't volunteer, the name of the restaurant. I figured that they would be too polite to object even if they hated Greek cuisine.

The conversation during the forty minutes it took for me to maneuver my little Toyota from Via Coronel to lower Sixth Street in San Pedro was light and cordial. No one mentioned anything about the murder, or the Triad. We were going to wait until the detectives had a couple of drinks before mentioning those subjects.

When I made my turn off of Gaffey Street in San Pedro, which the locals pronounce Peedro rather than the Spanish pronunciation with a hard "a" I was greeted by a central business area in transition. Bill explained that San Pedro had been in that same transition for as long as he could remember. It was like they couldn't make up their minds if they were going to renovate the entire place or skip every other block. On one block there would be some fairly nice retail establishments while another consisted of boarded up storefronts.

I listened while Bill explained the area to our guests.

"San Pedro," said Bill, "is a part of the City of Los Angeles and has a large Portuguese population. This is where its reputation as a fishing center comes from. Now, however, its biggest industry is the Port of Los Angeles, which employs over 247,000 people in Southern California." Showing that he had done his homework, he further added, "Over 2.6 million tons of goods, worth an excess of $11.5 billion, go through the port in a year to trade with China."

While I guided the car into the parking lot, Bill was explaining that the city also was the home of Fort Macarthur. It was named in honor of Lt. General Arthur Macarthur, the father of General Douglas Macarthur, who commanded the American forces in the Pacific during World War II.

During Bill's entire litany, the two men had not said a word.

The moment we opened the door to the restaurant, my hopes for a quiet dinner where we could talk were destroyed. In the lobby there was this big Greek guy greeting all of the women with kisses and pumping the hands of the men and pounding them on the back. I wasn't sure if this was a test of physical stamina or a traditional Greek greeting. Either way, we must have passed because we were taken to a table.

There was one large brightly lighted room with tables, no booths. On our way to the rear of the room where our table was located, we passed two well-known screen personalities with their families. No one was hounding them for autographs, so I figured that this must be a place the jaded locals go to avoid tourists.

The food was Greek all right. Dishes of lamb and grape leaves around anything that could be rolled. That didn't faze our Chinese guests in the least. They deferred the ordering to Bill and then ate the lamb and grape leaves with all the gusto of a K-Mart shopper during a blue light special. Their ferocious appetites were only exceeded by their thirst. Both of them inhaled their beers while my arm was still trying to decipher the signal from my brain to bend my elbow.

A quick glance at Bill's frantic expression told me that he was reading the situation similarly. This might be a business expense, but combining the prices of the food with what was shaping up to be a case of beer at restaurant prices, the tab for the evening was heading in the direction of the national debt.

In addition, the set-up in the dining room wasn't conducive to a business conversation along the lines we had planned, so the talk continued to consist of meaningless chatter. Much to his credit, Bill had learned to master small talk. His approach was simple. Get the subjects to talk about themselves. It hardly ever fails. A well placed question here, and another there, along with an expression of interest is all that it takes, and Bill was doing an outstanding job.

Mercifully, the hum of conversations around us was broken by the sound of music with a primal rap cadence that is as distinctly Greek as Oom-pah-pah is German.

At the rear of the room, the waiters discarded their trays and hustled to form a line. They stood side by side with arms extended on one another's shoulders. The music intensified and the dancers began kicking their legs in the air as they swayed to and fro in unison, while the patrons clapped in time with the music.

The dance completed, each took a glass from a nearby table, took a drink and threw the glasses on the floor where they shattered.

During the entertainment, I alternated between watching the dancers and our guests. They were as caught up in the moment as the regulars and were enthusiastically clapping, swaying and smiling. The evening was shaping up to be a success.

During one of our trips to the rest room, Bill and I decided that since we couldn't talk at our table, we would stop off at a more private place to have our conversation. We couldn't go to Bill's place since it didn't appear that our guests would be happy with Arrowhead bottled water. I suggested we go to a bar at one of the local hotels. This being a weeknight, the only people there would be businessmen talking business and sucking up to other businessmen. Bill suggested one a couple of streets over.

The cocktail lounge we went to was the exact opposite of the Papadakis Taverna. Except for the bartender, the place was deserted. We found a booth at the far end and ordered drinks. The two detectives stayed with beer. Bill stayed with water. I switched to straight club soda. One more beer and I was going to start sloshing.

As soon as the bartender was out of earshot, I started the conversation with, "We would like to talk with you about the situation we are working on together. First, my friend and I would like to know if you have identified the person in the house as being the individual you are looking for?"

Teng stole a look at Chen, who answered. "Mr. Tse has arranged to have several people he trusts enter the establishment. They will take pictures for us to look at. But at this time we still cannot say for sure."

I leaned toward them, my serious gaze covering both Chen and Teng. "And assuming that it is the right person, how do you intend to proceed? To our knowledge he hasn't broken any laws in the United States for which he could be arrested, and I don't believe the United States would extradite him to China. Even if they did, it would take a considerable amount of time."

My forthright question and comment caused some wriggling in their seats. This was fine. I was used to people being uncomfortable when I was questioning them. It was always to my advantage when they were. It wasn't just how they answered the question that gave me answers. Their body language usually told me just as much as the spoken word.

After a long silence during which neither Bill nor I uttered so much as a grunt, Chen answered. "We do not see where the United States authorities would have to be involved with our taking him back to China to stand trial for his crimes in that country."

Bill asked. "So you have made arrangements, should the need arise?"

"That has been done, yes," Chen replied.

"And may I ask how you will get the person out of the house to those arrangements," I inquired. "It will have to be done discreetly, as he would have every right to seek the help of the local police, since they don't know you are here."

Chen looked directly into my eyes. When he spoke, his voice was low and distinctly sharp. "We will find a way."

Bill chimed in, softening the tone the conversation was taking. "Mr. Chen and Mr. Teng, we are not the authorities and certainly won't compromise your situation in any way. However, our story is the murder of Susan McCloskey. We happen to believe that the conclusion to that story lies in the house of the person you are after. He, or someone, who is associated with him, is responsible for that murder. That is the person we want to expose. Our interest is in working with you to accomplish that task. What you do with the person you are after is your business. Not ours."

I could see the relief on Chen's face as he relaxed. "You have been very helpful to us. We will, of course, continue to work with you. I assure you, if you have not found an answer to your question before we have him back in Hong Kong, we will extract that information from him there and see that you get it. That is our commitment to you."

I believed him. I didn't want to know how the information was going to be wrung out of the guy, but I had every confidence that it would be. I could tell by the look on Bill's face that the thought of knowing how this was going to be accomplished didn't particularly appeal to him either.

Bill pulled an envelope out of his pocket and gave it to Chen. "I have some other fingerprints that we would appreciate your sending back to your country for identification."

As Chen reached for it, I told him whose they were and the story behind them. Chen handed them to Teng and said, "They will go out tomorrow by courier. I will be informed within two days if they are identified, which I am sure they will be."

"Wonderful," I said. "We appreciate that." I raised my glass. "Let's drink to a continuing trusting relationship, and may this mess be over very soon."

CHAPTER THIRTEEN

I started the new day feeling like a distance runner on the day of the big race. The finish line was in my sights, causing my adrenalin to pump like a West Texas oilrig. The previous night had validated the course of action I was taking.

As I was sitting on the patio, in my early morning shorts and tee shirt, sipping on a cup of hot tea, the only thing that bothered me was, the story that appeared to be coming out of it. I personally always had the philosophy that you told it like it was and let the chips fall where they may. However, Bill had his life savings tied up in a local paper. In this era of nauseating sensitivity to anything remotely ethnic, he could well be accused of Asian bashing.

Rather than let something as mundane as a conscience spoil my day, I decided to write it as I saw it and let Bill do the worrying. Sun Fu Yee hadn't yet returned my call, so I decided to shower, then call him.

Just as I was on my way up the stairs the phone rang. I let the answering machine get it. It was Lucinda wondering why I hadn't called her, and asking if I had any information about the fingerprints she had gotten for me.

Shower completed, I placed my call to Yee. I thought I

was going to get the answering machine again when a drowsy voice answered. I identified myself and marveled at how quickly someone could get the sleep out of his voice. He apologized for not returning my call, but didn't offer an explanation. That was fine. It probably would have been a concocted excuse anyway. I asked him if we could get together as I had something I wanted to discuss with him in person. He suggested we meet at the paper. After a brief pause, he said he could be there between 9:30 and 9:45, depending on traffic.

Before we left for the office, Bill and I agreed, since the talk with Yee was going to be billed as being off the record, that it might be less threatening to him if I met with him alone. He was FBI and, although he cooperated with Stan, from my brief dealings with the Bureau, they were victims of the Washington bureaucracy in that the required ream of paper documentation usually accompanied every meeting.

Sun Fu Yee arrived five minutes early.

After the brief obligatory Southern California laid back salutations of "How ya doing?" "Hanging in there," we made our way, coffee from the backroom in hand, to the conference room where I closed the door and we took our favorite chairs.

From the outset, I sensed that Yee wasn't acting his usual, I'm-a-hip-and-carefree-dude personality. His face was tighter and his movements were more deliberate than in our previous meetings. I detected that Sun Fu Yee the thespian was being replaced by Sun Fu Yee the Federal Agent, and we were going to talk serious stuff. That made it much easier for me to say what I was going to say.

"I asked that we meet because Stan told me that you're

with the Bureau. That puts us on a more level playing field. You've always known what I do, but I didn't know what you did. I want us to agree that unless we specifically say otherwise, our conversation is strictly off the record."

Yee looked at me over the rim of his coffee cup as he slowly took another swallow. It wasn't until he put it back on the table that he replied. "It's much easier for you to say than for me. If I find something that clearly impacts an ongoing investigation that I know about, I have to use it. I doubt very seriously that you can tell me anything I don't already know, or have some idea about. All I can promise is that if I see us getting into that realm, I'll stop you and let you know. Is that agreed?"

No dummy, this guy. But as Stan had said earlier, he played it square. He laid out the rules he was willing to play by, then placed the ball back in my court. I could reject his rules and the meeting would be over, or I could play by them and see where we headed. I decided to play. "Agreed. You want to tell me what you know that I don't think you know, to get the ball rolling?"

He briefly reverted to the old Yee and actually let himself smile. "For starters, I know that you have been working with two detectives from China who are staying at the home of a man named Tse in Palos Verdes. They are watching a house directly across from the Tse house. They believe its occupant to be a Triad leader who has a false identity. They would desperately like to get him back to Hong Kong to extract a measure of justice out of his hide."

As Yee was talking, I could feel my poker face abandoning me.

Yee saw it too. "I also know that you gave fingerprints supposedly taken from the deceased to them. They told you that they belonged to the Triad leader's mistress. I find it interesting that he would have his mistress marry someone else. That is so unlike the Chinese. They don't like to share their possessions, particularly their mistresses. Anyhow, I also know that you had dinner last night with the two gentlemen in San Pedro. How am I doing?"

Raising my eyebrows a twitch, I replied, "So far you've convinced me that you're either tailing me or the Hong Kong detectives, or you have a bug hidden somewhere."

"Since we're off the record, I admit to your being right on both counts. But to set the record straight, the bug isn't on you or your paper. Again, off the record, I owe you an explanation. My assignment here is as a part of the Justice Department investigation regarding illegal campaign contributions."

He was referring to the alleged illegal contributions made to the Democratic National Committee, including the infamous fundraiser held at the Buddhist Temple starring the previous Vice President of the United States. "Since I'm one of the few Chinese-Americans in the Bureau who's a field operative and not an inside accountant, I was one of the chosen few to be sent undercover. When Stan called me about you, I jumped at the chance to see what you had. As soon as I found out about the picture in the travel agency, and then what happened to Sidney Lu, I was authorized to follow this part of the case to see if there was a connection between our active investigation and yours."

"And your conclusion?" I probed.

"I found several of the players to be active in both." He got up from his chair as he finished the sentence. "But rather than continuing right now, could you meet with me downtown this evening? I think you'll find it worthwhile, and things will become clearer for you."

I was puzzled, but agreed to meet him at the Biltmore Towers. Carleton Yang had his offices in the same building. He told me not to tell anyone I was meeting him. My years in Chicago had taught me to always let someone know where I was and what I was up to. He agreed that I could tell Bill.

The balance of the afternoon was spent doing nothing. I resisted the urge to call Lucinda. Since she had gone to visit her sister, my sex life had been in limbo. Nothing new there. When it came to sex I bounced between starvation and gluttony. I did the next best thing. I went back to Bill's and lay out on the patio.

Yee had insisted that I be at the room in the Towers no later than six that evening. He was adamant that, should I be late, I should not come at all. With that admonishment still fresh in my mind, I allowed myself two hours to get from the Peninsula to downtown. I was knocking on the office door by five.

Yee didn't even mention I was early after admitting me to the waiting room of an unoccupied office suite. "We can talk freely," he said. "We're the only ones here."

That remark made me feel like I was committing adultery. The feeling was reinforced as I followed him down a corridor of vacant offices into the corner office.

My adulterous mood passed quickly when I surveyed the room. To anyone who has ever watched a crime show on television, or seen a movie, it was immediately obvious what the office was being used for, and it wasn't clandestine sex. The first clue was the sophisticated monitoring equipment. The second was the empty Burger King paper bags that were being used as wastebaskets.

Absent were ashtrays with partially smoked cigarette butts in them. I guessed OSHA had infiltrated the FBI, and they had gone smokeless in the workplace.

"I guess by now you've guessed what this is?" said Yee.

"Looks like something straight out of Law and Order."

Yee pointed to one of the two folding chairs by the table. "Have a seat. We're going to be the only ones here. With the grand jury's indictment of Mr. Chan, the primary suspect in the Democratic National Committee illegal campaign contribution probe, this tap has officially and legally come to an end and I've been ordered to disband. However, the group we've been monitoring is meeting again tonight and I want to hear what they have to say. I think you will, too. Since the investigation is over, I've turned off the tape. So if you want to remember anything, off the record, of course, you had better take notes."

"You mind filling me in a little more, so I know what I'm listening for?"

I sat back in the chair and listened as Special Agent Yee paced the floor and began an unbelievable tale. As I suspected, the tap was in Carleton Yang's office. It started because Carleton Yang had been identified many years ago as a large Democratic Party contributor and Asian activist. He was a power broker in the Asian community, a strong voting bloc for Los Angeles county Democratic office seekers. He was also known to associate with those under investigation for illegal fundraising and alleged attempts by the Chinese government to influence the American presidential elections.

Yee stopped for a moment. "I'm telling you this part, only as background information. This is as far as I'm going to go because it's still an officially open case."

"Understand," I assured him.

He went on to tell me that, as a result of the surveillance, they had found out that a group of influential Asian businessmen, whom the eavesdroppers referred to as the Council of Elders, were meeting twice a month to chart the future of the Los Angeles Asian community.

"There is nothing illegal about people meeting this way," said Yee, "and there was never anything they said that in any way pointed to an objective that they were plotting to overthrow the Government.

"Mr. Tse is a member of the council. The group spent most of their time talking about issues facing the various Asian communities in the Los Angeles/Orange County areas. When I say Asian, I'm speaking about the whole enchilada—Chinese, Korean, and Japanese—although they excluded the Vietnamese and Cambodians. One of the Filipino elected officials from Gardena, I believe, was involved."

I interrupted him to ask what made Gardena, a community close to the city of Torrance, so important that they would bring in a politician from there. He told me that Gardena was a city that was almost totally controlled politically by people of Asian descent.

Yee said that listening to the group was like sitting in on a meeting of a local town council. They had both long-range objectives and short range goals. For example, they had a committee to identify younger politicians to groom for city council and mayor of some of the larger municipalities, then later for statewide office. They were all very aware of the demographics. After a UCLA study showed that Torrance would be sixty percent Asian in a very short time, they targeted that city for an Asian mayor.

What piqued Yee's interest had to do more with the short-term. The council had discussed the increasing Triad and Tong activity. Small shop owners were being charged protection money and were afraid to go to the local authorities, fearing that their shops would be burned down and they would be killed.

Just listening to Yee do so much talking made my mouth feel dry. I saw a small refrigerator standing in one corner of the room and, during one of his pauses, asked if he had anything in it to drink. He told me to help myself to whatever was there. I helped myself to a can of diet Coke and returned to the chair, once again, giving Yee my undivided attention.

He went on without missing a pronoun. During one of their discussions, Yee had found out that I was not only working with him, but that I had also seen Carleton Yang. The Elders were very interested in what I was digging up and had voted to cooperate with me, although they were concerned that what I wrote would spark fear and resentment among the non-Asian population. When I came up with the picture of the Triad, and Yang contacted his friends in Hong Kong, it had caused quite a stir. Yang had been at the fund-raiser and had met the man, as had some of the others, but had no idea who he was at the time. They took him as just another Hong Kong businessman who elected to leave before the communist government took control.

Yee abruptly stopped talking as a faint sound came from one of the amplifiers. "Someone's coming into the conference room where we have the bug," he said. "That'll be Yang's assistant setting out the agenda. They're very organized. I wish our staff meetings at the Bureau were as orderly. I guarantee the meeting will start in precisely ten minutes, so if you have to relieve yourself, do it now. The key to the john's over there, on the hook."

"I think I'll take you up on it," I replied as I made my way to the door.

When I returned, Yee motioned me to have a seat. "They're ready to begin. Yang just welcomed everyone. Get comfortable. Once they get going, they don't stop."

"I hope this is in English."

"It is. Everyone in the room may be of Asian descent, but that doesn't mean they all understand each other's language. They could probably all read it because most of the characters are the same in the different Asian languages, but that's about it."

I took a seat as he turned up the volume. The unmistakable high-pitched voice of Carleton Yang was heard telling the group that the main topic for the meeting was the problem in Palos Verdes. Mr. Tse would give that report.

Listening to Tse, I could picture him posing like an Oriental Napoleon as he had at his house. His report was surprisingly short. He told them that after he had met with me (whom he referred to as the reporter from Chicago), and was told where the Triad leader lived, he'd arranged for a trusted person to work for the gardener. He had also arranged to have the driver of the truck that delivered fresh vegetables to the house every day secretly take pictures of whomever he saw there. He had circulated pictures of the Triad leader among the trusted, and two people had confirmed that the man was indeed living there.

He went on to say that the two detectives from Hong

Kong had wired their findings to their superiors in Hong Kong and were waiting for instructions.

A strange voice interrupted to ask if Tse had any idea of the alternatives they were looking at.

Yee said, "That's the voice of one of the local politicians."

Tse continued. "My household staff have reported that they are discussing ways to take him out of the country for a public trial, or how they could eliminate him here if that is the order."

The politician and several others chimed in to object to the latter course. "We do not need another killing here," said the politician.

Another voice echoed the sentiment. "I don't object to killing him, but the Chicago reporter has already alarmed the people about gang activity, and to have another murder would do much harm to our image. We must keep our long-range objectives in mind. To have another killing that is tied to organized crime will only give the conservative politicians more fuel to pass laws halting immigration."

Yee smiled as he looked over at me. "Hear how famous you are?"

I laughed back. "You guys have a hard time understanding it, but it's true, the pen is greater than the sword. Let this be a lesson to you."

"You're preaching to the choir here, my friend," he replied.

Stan had told me that Yee was one of his "unnamed sources." This young man knew how to use the press to his advantage, just as he was doing with me now, although I wasn't quite sure yet what he had in mind.

Our attention instantly reverted back to the speaker as

we both recognized the unmistakable voice of Carleton Yang. "We must persuade the people in China that killing the Triad Leader in the United States would be a grievous mistake. Taking him out of the country will not be noticed by anyone, but a killing here would be thoroughly investigated by the authorities."

There was a pause in the conversation when a voice I had not heard before spoke. From the look on his face, I could tell that Yee didn't recognize the voice either.

"We know that it can be arranged," said the voice. "As we have learned on many occasions, it is only the amount of money that it will take. The higher level authority that must make the decision determines the amount. In this case, the authority is very high in the government, so we are talking thousands of dollars."

It was Yang again. "It is agreed then that we will begin the negotiations."

We heard what sounded like a bunch of grunts, then Yang spoke once more. "I will begin the negotiations immediately."

Yee looked at his watch and then turned off the switch. "They'll be adjourning in about five minutes."

"How do you know?"

"Because Yang's as crafty a person as you're ever going to meet. As soon as he gets the decision he wants, he adjourns the meeting before there can be any further discussion. He comes in with one agenda, manipulates things around until that agenda is completed, defers everything else until the next meeting and then adjourns. Since they stagger their departure times, we had better get the hell out of here while we can."

We turned off the lights and left the room. We had no

trouble getting an elevator and were soon retrieving our respective cars out of the garage.

The ride home was scary because I didn't remember anything about it. My mind was so busy churning over the evening that I didn't spend a second on driving. Luckily for me, traffic on the Harbor Freeway was unusually light. For the umpteenth time, I muddled over in my mind the twists and turns that this case had taken in just a few short weeks. We went from a simple murder to Triads and Tongs, a plan to virtually take over the political process in California, involvement in an FBI wiretap, stolen identities, and Chinese detectives. That reminded me of Detective Bilbo. He had been very quiet.

There had been virtually no ink from either the *Breeze* or the *Times* regarding the murder. From the lack of letters to the editor, the general public seemed indifferent as well.

Looking at it pragmatically, if we were going to sell papers, we had to have something more sensational, keeping our stories murder-centered. Good stories aren't worth the paper they're printed on if no one bothers to read them.

Bill wanted to know what happened the moment I came through the door. I started to tell him the story as I made my way to the fridge to get a bottle of water. Neither one of us bothered to sit, and Bill didn't interrupt until I finished telling him everything I remembered. Although I had taken out my note pad in the hotel room I hadn't bothered to write anything down. There was nothing during the conversation that I couldn't remember and write out later at home.

After my monologue, we moved from the kitchen to the living room. I could see Bill processing everything that I had told him. "So, where do we go from here?" he asked.

"I guess we just go with the flow, except that we have to keep closely in touch with our two detective friends. It's obvious the Elders weren't sure of how much we should be involved. We either have to get closer to the two Chinese detectives or find another way to assure that we're in when the curtain starts to go down."

Before Bill could reply, I asked if he had heard anything from Bilbo. He shook his head no.

Another plan was beginning to formulate in my fertile mind. We could screw around with all the little people but, to get something done, you have to go to the person who can make the decision. In this case it was Carleton Yang. I outlined my plan to Bill. He didn't agree with it totally, but he had no better alternative. We agreed that I'd call Yang in the morning and set up a meeting that same day, as things were moving fast. I was sure that Yang had already called Hong Kong.

We also agreed that we would need Detective Bilbo's help soon. Legal authority would be needed to open doors, and, most importantly, make an arrest, which is the only way we could publish the story.

As much as my loins told me to telephone Lucinda now, my mind wasn't on the same track. I decided to call her in the morning, and retired for the night. I don't even remember closing my eyes.

CHAPTER FOURTEEN

Yet, another day sneaked up on me. I may even have set a personal record for sleeping through the night. My exhaustion didn't surprise me. It was purely emotional and happened every time I worked on a good story that was about to be resolved. I would go through this until the final draft was written and then, when I saw the finished product on the newsstands, there would be an ensuing rush of adrenaline and it would be history. Then on to the next one. Such is the life of someone in my profession.

I eased into the morning by having a cup of hot tea on the patio while Bill went for his morning bicycle ride. I took the initiative early. It was still too early to call Carleton Yang, but I stood a good chance of getting to Detective Bilbo.

Bilbo was in the office. Man, I thought, I'm really going to ruin your day. His greeting was very cordial. We chatted briefly about my stay in PV, and he said that there was still nothing new on the case. I told him I didn't call for that reason. Before he had a chance to ask me, I asked him my first tantalizing question. "How long would it take you to get a search warrant?" Before he could answer, I followed with, "And on a scale of one to five, with one being extremely difficult, how do the judges around here lean?"

He was silent for awhile, then said, "What do you have in mind?"

I was ready with an even more evasive answer, calculated to make him drool on his tie. "Let's just say that I may have something on very short notice. If you can get a search warrant quick enough, it could lead to an arrest that solves the case."

He paused again. "You know it's against the law to withhold evidence. You can get in a lot of trouble."

I needed him or I would have replied, *At least someone is gathering evidence, which is more than I can say for the Palos Verdes Estates Police Department.* Instead, I used all my will power and tactfully told him that if I wanted to withhold evidence and take credit for solving the case, I wouldn't be on the telephone with him.

He admitted that they could get a warrant within an hour. He didn't bother to hide the anxiety in his voice when he replied, "If you can give me a rough idea of what we're talking about, I can get my Chief on board and we can do some preliminary skid greasing. If you can give us a general time frame, it would speed things up even more. Then we could be sure the Judge we want would be available."

"Sorry," I answered, enjoying the posturing. "I'm at the mercy of other people on this. This could happen anytime between this afternoon and day after tomorrow. To be on the safe side, Bill will always be reachable. I think it would be prudent that you two know how to reach one another on exceedingly short notice."

He would have kept me on the phone all day probing, so I cut the conversation off quickly with a, "Gotta go.

Talk to you later," and hung up on him. Ten to one that he was swearing, and twenty to one that he was in with his Chief before I had a chance to tell Bill, who was just coming through the door.

When I told him about Bilbo's reaction, Bill laughed so hard I thought he was going to pee his pants. "I can just see him now," said Bill, "coffee dripping off his mustache, tripping over the waste basket as he made a beeline to the Chief's office. They'll spend the next twenty minutes cursing you. Then they'll brainstorm trying to figure out what you were talking about so they could beat you to it. Then they'll try to decide what to say to the judge because they can't afford not to."

By the time I got dressed, it was time to make my call to Carleton Yang. Bill eavesdropped on my conversation. He must have been disappointed because Carleton came on the phone almost immediately and, sensing the urgency in my voice, asked if I could come right over. I agreed to do so.

But I made a mistake a native Los Angeleno rarely makes, agreeing to meet someone downtown Los Angeles during the early morning commute hours. I soon found myself sitting in one of the infamous LA traffic jams on the Harbor Freeway. The one-hour drive ended two-and-a half-hours later, compliments of a series of fender benders expertly spaced to assure maximum congestion.

I was ushered into Carleton Yang's inner office the moment I arrived. Carleton came from behind his ornate desk to shake my hand and motioned me to join him at the conversation area in the corner of the room, where we were served coffee and tea. Carleton was his usual courteous, suave self as he asked me how I had been. I told him I was fine, but that the case was, in my mind, coming to a close and I wished to talk with him about coordinating my paper's efforts with the detectives from Hong Kong.

While I showed my anxiety by leaning forward and extending my hands outward while I was speaking, Yang was totally in control of his emotions. "I have been assured by the gentlemen from Hong Kong that they are fully cooperating with you. But they are representatives of the Chinese authorities and there is little I can do except to voice my desire that they continue to do so."

I got to the point. "Mr. Yang, I have appreciated your help since I first came to see you. Without your assistance, I would be in the same place the local authorities are in, which is nowhere. But now, we both know that the Triad leader has been located, since I was the one who found him. We also know that the detectives from Hong Kong are here without the knowledge of the United States authorities. Except for being in the country under false pretenses, the Triad leader has not broken any local laws. Given this, the detectives have two choices. They will either try and smuggle him back out of the country, or eliminate him here."

He did no more than nod his head.

"Do you agree with me so far?" I asked him, to get some sort of reaction.

He bowed his head a little further.

"The latter," I continued, "would be most unfortunate. It would not be good public relations for the Chinese community in Los Angeles." I paused and poured myself coffee. This type of action usually resulted in a verbal response from the other party if they were Caucasian. Anglos can't stand silence in the midst of conversations and always fill in the space. Reporters and interviewers rely on this when digging for information. Carleton Yang merely sat there and waited for me to proceed.

"The key to solving the murder lies with the man the detectives want. To remove him without his supplying us with that information will take away any hope that the authorities will be able to find and punish the murderer. It will also force me," I paused for effect, "to concentrate on the Triad, the leader's disappearance or elimination, the fact that two Hong Kong detectives were here, where they stayed, along with pictures of them coming out of his house," a bluff, but Yang didn't know it, "and other information that I have."

For the first time, Yang reacted. He folded his hands together and placed the tip of his fingers under his chin. "That would be most unfortunate."

I felt like I had just scored a major victory and allowed myself the luxury of sitting back in the chair and crossing my legs.

"Yes it would," I agreed, "particularly since it can be avoided."

"I will do what I can to see that you get your story."

I was sure we understood one another now, so considered it safe to impart another piece of information that I wanted the detectives to know. I told Yang about the severed ears.

He nodded his head quickly, and said, "I will ask the detectives if that is a trademark of any of the assassins they know."

"I asked them before," I reminded him. "If they knew of any trademarks of the Triad's known killers and, since they haven't gotten back to me, I've assumed they haven't come up with any information."

"I will find out," said Yang, "and call you with my findings."

Before leaving, I made one final demand. "I will give the detectives a number where I can always be reached. I must know immediately when they remove the leader from his house. They must get the information about the woman's killing and relay that information either before they remove him, or soon thereafter. If there is evidence in the house, I must know where to find it, so that our authorities can use it. This is important to my emphasizing the murder itself and not the fact that the good people of Palos Verdes have Triads living among them."

I got up to leave.

Yang also got up from his chair and said, "I understand and will make sure that message is also understood by Mr. Chen and Mr. Teng."

As we passed his desk on the way toward the door, he stopped and picked up an envelope. "This is the information on the fingerprints you asked us to get from China. I think you will find it most interesting."

I opened it, read the short note inside, and said, "You'll find it more interesting when you find out who these are from." I quickly told the story.

"That explains much," he said.

I glanced at a photograph that rested on a back credenza. You Wiley old bastard, I thought, as I left his office.

The ride back to Palos Verdes was much better. I made it unscathed through the I-10 freeway interchange. A masochist posing as a traffic engineer must have laid out the Harbor Freeway. I had heard somewhere that the Santa

Monica Freeway in that area was the busiest in the world. If the traffic at 11:45 AM is any indication, that rumor is true. The only way you can make it from the on ramp into the left-hand lanes is to put on the turn signal and a diaper and just do it. I did it, made it, and miraculously ended up back in Palos Verdes in less than an hour.

I went directly to Bill's house, phoning him as soon as I was back. Then I called Lucinda. Since I had given Bill's number to Carleton Yang, I had to decline her invitation to meet at her apartment. I almost asked her to come over, but thought better of it. Bill had never volunteered me the use of his home to bring a guest, and I really didn't want her there when the call to action came. We chatted for a while before I told her that Bill didn't have call waiting and I had to keep the telephone line open. She wasn't too happy about that, but such is life in the fast lane. There was nothing more I could do but wait, and there was no better place than the patio on the chaise.

It was exactly 7:59 PM, and Bill had just turned to AMC to catch an old movie that we had last seen with our dates when we were both in college. The phone rang. It was Mr. Tse telling me that his driver would pick me up in fifteen minutes.

I jumped up from the couch and ran up the stairs to my room for my notebook.

The television was still on, but Bill wasn't watching it. "I'll be by the phone until you return," he said with a concerned look on his face. "I don't like this one bit."

"You better telephone Bilbo to stay by his phone, too. I'll be all right." I hoped I sounded more convincing than I felt.

DEATH ON THE HILL

By the time I reached the front sidewalk, the adrenaline was really pumping.

Anxiety replaced initial trepidation. I didn't have much time to think about it, as Tse's Lincoln rolled into view, stopping directly in front of me. I waved to Bill as the back door swung open and I crouched to get in. As the car sped away, I looked out the back window to see Bill writing down the license number.

In the back seat with me was the same bodyguard who had escorted me to the Tse house for the first time. "What's going on?"

His only response was to give me a mask. "You have to put this on."

"I don't want to."

"Mr. Tse said if you won't wear it, we are to turn the car around and take you back."

I pulled the mask over my eyes without comment. I tried to determine how well I could see around the mask. I was sightless. Rather than fight it, I leaned my head back against the seat and closed my eyes to concentrate on my hearing as I had seen Sean Connery do in a James Bond film. It didn't work. I couldn't hear a thing. Damn. Where was Ian Fleming when I needed him most.

I guessed we had been riding for around a half-hour. Several times I thought I heard aircraft. We seemed close to the airport, which stands to reason if you are going to smuggle someone out of the country.

After several sharp turns, the Lincoln came to an abrupt halt. Only then, did my traveling companion sitting next to me speak. "Wait," he said. "I will come around and help you out. Please don't try to remove your eye covering until you are told."

The door opened, and I felt his hand on my arm as he guided me out of the vehicle. As I was being turned around, I felt a second hand on my other arm. The driver must have joined the bodyguard. We stopped, I heard a knock, and someone inside called out in Chinese. After one of my escorts responded in Chinese, the door opened and I was ushered inside. The hands on my arms guided me forward.

From underneath the mask, I saw light for the first time. I felt the hands of my escorts relax their grip as a familiar voice told me it was okay to remove the mask. At first, the light blinded me. But soon, I was able to distinguish the face of Mr. Chen smiling in front of me. He apologized for the inconvenience, and asked that I follow him.

I looked around the room, which seemed like some sort of restaurant supply storage room. Not surprising, since Tse was in that business.

Walking into the next room, a musty odor greeted me. My flesh felt like insects were crawling over my entire body. I felt like I entered a medieval torture chamber. This feeling was reinforced when I observed an unfamiliar figure, sitting in an armchair with a sheet draped around his torso. I was sure I was looking at the infamous Chinese Triad Chief. I took a better look to see if I could recognize the man I had seen in the photograph. As I crept closer I saw that his arms were tied to the arms of the chair. Blood was oozing from under his fingernails. It almost turned my stomach when I realized what was happening. I had read about Chinese torture methods before, and I was staring at one of the most gruesome. Blood encrusted splinters of wood protruded from under the victim's fingernails. It wasn't a pleasant sight.

I looked into a face wracked with pain. His eyes were glazed over and he seemed to be in a trance. But even so, there was no doubt that this was the same man.

Chen said, "Mister Jung has something to tell you." He went over to the bound figure and put his hand under the man's chin causing him to raise his head. Chen bent down until the two figures were nose to nose and spoke to the man in Chinese.

In halting English, the vanquished and broken Triad chieftain told me his story. Several times during the next half-hour, I requested that his captors give him water, which they did reluctantly. I listened to the tale unfold, interrupting for clarification, and to verify that he was telling the truth. It surprised me how much I was piecing together. When he finished, his head slumped forward, his chin resting on his chest in a faint. I thought he was dead, and my insistence on learning who had killed Susan McCloskey had caused him to be tortured to death. Looking closer, I saw his chest was still heaving.

Mr. Teng appeared at my side. "It is unfortunate, but necessary for us to get the information you needed. It is nothing more than he has done to many others, many times."

Teng must have noticed that I was looking a little queasy because he took me into a small adjoining office. He guided me to a chair and Mr. Chen handed me a glass of water. I deliberately avoided looking too closely at my surroundings, for if it ever came to my being asked to describe the place, it would be easy to say I couldn't and mean it.

"How did you manage to get the Triad from his PV

fortress?" I asked Chen.

He proudly explained how it had been accomplished. Every Monday at exactly 9:30 AM, Don Yee, the Triad's gardener, arrived at the iron gates of the mansion on Via Coronel. On the morning in question, the guards automatically waved the truck through without noticing that Yee had a new helper. That helper had been detective Chen. Yee had driven to the back of the house, parking his truck next to the rose garden. Then Chen and Yee had unloaded their lawnmowers and had started cutting the lawn. A half-hour later, they'd loaded two large plastic bags of grass clippings into the back of the truck.

While they were busy pruning the rose bushes, the Triad chief emerged from the back door of the mansion. When planning the venture, Yee had told Chen that the Triad chief never varied his routine. He always took a morning walk in his rose garden, then sat for at least a half-hour in the gazebo.

The Triad chief didn't notice Chen working his way toward the gazebo. Grabbing the Triad from behind, Chen had located a pressure point behind his temple, which, when pressed, would render him unconscious. In a matter of seconds, the Triad slumped in Chen's arms without uttering a sound. Yee joined the detective and had helped him place the unconscious figure beneath the bags of grass clippings. The drive out of the estate had been as uneventful as their entrance.

Detective Teng was waiting for the truck as it arrived at Tse's estate. The unconscious body of the Triad was given a precautionary tranquilizer shot before being transferred into a waiting van.

Within an hour the two detectives had the conscious,

but still groggy, Triad tied to a chair in a room at one of Tse's warehouses near Los Angeles International Airport. All the arrangements had been made to spirit the Triad back to Hong Kong, but first, they had to honor their commitment to the American journalist to provide him with information about Susan McCloskey's murder.

The Triad's initial reluctance to part with any information helpful to the detectives lasted longer than the detectives had anticipated. It was only after they relied upon an ancient, but effective, torture technique that he told them what they wanted to know.

After Chen completed his story, Teng spoke again. "If you have everything you need, the driver will take you back."

I was more than happy to get out of there, but first, I asked Teng what he was going to do with the man in the other room.

"He will be taken back to China within the hour," Teng replied.

I got the impression that there was one piece of cargo that might disappear over the Pacific Ocean. Before leaving, I asked to use the telephone. I could see the reluctance on the faces of my hosts, so I told them that Bill wanted me to call him to be sure I was all right. Teng gave me permission after I said they could listen to my conversation.

Bill answered on the first ring. I told him that I was fine and would be leaving in a few minutes. As an after thought, I added, "I'm looking forward to being back with you and Bilbo." I hoped he would call the detective and have him there when I arrived. It was important that Bilbo get into the Triad's house as quickly as possible.

I shook hands with the two detectives and tried not to look at the figure slumped over in the chair as I left. I donned my mask before being whisked out to the waiting Lincoln. Unlike the earlier trip, the bodyguard and driver carried on a conversation in Chinese. There was also quite a bit of laughter, although I didn't see what they found so funny. I knew that I wouldn't forget what I had seen, and guaranteed that, if I ever went to China, I sure as hell wouldn't break any laws.

Maybe it was the constant chatter, but the return trip didn't seem to take as long. I knew when we arrived back on the Peninsula, and soon we were back at Bill's. This time my mask was taken off inside the car, and I was let out of the car down the street, rather than in front of the condo.

As I approached the condo, I recognized Bilbo's unmarked police car in one of the guest parking spots.

I had just put my hand on the doorknob, when a visibly relieved Bill opened it from the inside. "God, I'm glad you're back."

I had never been called God before, but I sure thanked him when I felt the warmth within the room. "So am I."

Standing in the middle of the room was Bilbo and an older, thinner man whom I hadn't seen since the crime scene at the McCloskey house. I shook hands with Bilbo as he turned toward the other man and introduced him as Greg Wilson, "his chief."

I didn't bother to sit down. "You guys ready to solve your crime? When you get the warrant to search that house on Via Coronel, you've got yourself an arrest."

"We'll get the warrant if you have something to tell us that will convince a Judge," the Chief answered sarcastically. "Do you mind telling us who we're going to arrest?"

I milked the moment as long as I could before I flippantly responded. "The husband. Who else?"

Neither policeman said a word. Both just stood there with the same blank look on their faces.

"Sit for a minute," I told them, heading for my favorite spot on the couch, "and I'll tell you what I have. But speed is of the essence here."

Bilbo took a seat beside me, the Chief took Bill's favorite chair, and Bill sat on a cushion on the floor. I started with the obvious, referring to the last article I wrote explaining the Triads. I tied the accident to my following the Asian woman to the house on Via Coronel. I explained how that had led to my guess that the Triad chief lived in that house. I also told them about the two Chinese detectives who had come into the country to find him after I had sent a picture that had been given to me to Hong Kong for identification. The Chief asked me where I got the picture, to which I said, "I can't disclose my sources."

I went on to say that the detectives had spirited the Triad Chief out of the country, but, before they did, they had grilled him, at my request, about the murder. During the interrogation, he had implicated McCloskey and told them where to find evidence that would prove McCloskey's involvement in his wife's murder.

I retrieved copies of the information I had gotten from the County Recorder's office from my room. Chief Wilson took the official looking paper the motherly clerk had given me, looked it over, and handed it to Bilbo.

"You'll notice," I said, "that the house the Triad leader lives in, is in McCloskey's name. That's when I first suspected that he was either involved in his wife's death, or knew who was responsible for it and why."

"There's no law against that," Bilbo piped in.

What a stupid comment, I thought. Chief Wilson's facial expression showed that he agreed with me.

"But add it to his having dinner at the Admiral Risty with the woman who lives in the house of a notorious underworld character while his wife's body is still warm, and even an amateur like myself begins to get suspicious."

I handed Wilson the envelope that Carleton Yang had given me about the fingerprints of the girl who had been with McCloskey at the Admiral Risty. I explained how I had gotten them.

Wilson couldn't believe it. "They're the same fingerprints as the murdered woman."

"That's right, and that's why I knew that McCloskey was a key player in his wife's death. He gave me the articles that supposedly were only touched by his wife."

"But why would he do that?" Bilbo asked. "It doesn't make any sense."

"Sure it does," the Chief said. "The Triad's mistress is here under an assumed identity, but she can't change the identity of her fingerprints, so here's a perfect opportunity to die and have the prints purged from police records."

"Exactly," I interjected. "Just a little insurance policy to bury her forever."

For the first time since I had started, Bill commented that it was an insurance policy that would be regretted for a long time by everyone concerned.

Bilbo still wasn't satisfied. I could see it on his face, so I asked what was wrong.

His reply was, "I still don't understand why Susan

McCloskey was killed. What was the motive?"

"I surmised from both the amount of cash in the wife's bank account, and what was found in her office, that she got too Americanized and ambitious and demanded more of the profits from their little alien smuggling ring."

"What smuggling ring? This is the first I've heard of a smuggling ring." Bilbo furrowed his brow and looked directly at me. "How do you know about the safe deposit box and what was in the files at the travel agency? We didn't find any cash there."

I had to resort to telling him part of the truth. "McCloskey told me about the cash, and the Hong Kong detectives told me tonight about the reason she was eliminated."

I continued with the story. "Chen had told me that Jung, the Triad chief, had told them that bringing in illegal aliens and giving them false identities was Susan Wong's idea. She was his mistress's niece and had run a travel business in Hong Kong. She was bankrolled by the Triad to set up a travel business in the States. From her previous dealings with U.S. authorities, she knew that once a person got into the States there was no accounting for their whereabouts. Knowing that Congress was about to pass a new law that made it mandatory for the U.S. Immigration Department to track foreign visitors and assure that they didn't stay in the country, she was anxious to make as much money as fast as she could before the law took effect.

"Since she also handled travel arrangements for United States citizens of Chinese ancestry coming into Hong Kong and then going into Communist China to visit relatives, it was a simple matter to pull past files, subscribe to newspapers in outlying areas that had Chinese-American communities, and read the obituaries. The families of the dead whose identities they took wouldn't say anything for fear their relative's back in their native provinces would be punished.

"The scheme worked so well that the Triad leader, who feared the Communist takeover of Hong Kong, decided to use it for himself to transfer his base of operations to the U.S. Marrying McCloskey was also a calculated move by Susan. She thought someone in the airline business would be helpful in illegal alien smuggling, and later, drug smuggling. In addition, she needed to find a front person to purchase items, such as the house in PV, so the Triad leader's new identity could remain anonymous. She was smart, but her ambition eventually did her in.

"The Triad leader didn't know what information she could take to the U.S. authorities for him to be deported back to a country where sure death awaited him. By making McCloskey arrange to kill his wife, he had a permanent hold on him. A bonus with Susan out of the way was that McCloskey could search for any damaging evidence the Triad chief thought Susan Wong had had. Like all thieves, the Chief didn't trust anyone, which is why he arranged the break-in at the travel agency offices to get the files. They contained the names of all the people they had brought into the country, who, incidentally, the gang continued to blackmail. Those poor bastards would be paying for the rest of their lives for fear they would be deported. A pretty nice racket. One that the Triad couldn't let an ambitious woman screw up."

When I finished, the room was silent.

Bilbo started to say something, but the Chief silenced

him. Finally, the Chief looked at Bilbo and said, "I think we have enough for a warrant."

As they were leaving, I said, "There's one more thing I forgot to tell you."

Both policemen stopped in their tracks.

I dropped my calculated bomb. "I happen to know exactly where to find the one piece of evidence that the DA will need to tie the noose, and I will be happy to lead you to it. But Bill and I will have to go with you."

Two hours later, at exactly 12:56 A.M., we were following three Palos Verdes Estates police cars and one Sheriff's car up Via Coronel. When we arrived at the estate, the gates were locked, but we could see lights on in the house.

Bilbo found the intercom and pushed the lighted button. He had to push it several times before a female voice responded. After identifying himself and stating that he had a search warrant to enter the premises, I checked my watch. It was 1:02 am.

At 1:06 am we watched as two Chinese men in jumpsuits came toward us in an electric golf cart. Seeing the police cars with their overhead lights on, the men quickly unlocked the gates and swung them open without checking the warrant that Bilbo held out.

Even in the dark, the entrance to the house was imposing. The Italian Cypresses that lined the drive were more monumental when silhouetted against a full moon, as they were tonight. As we drove up the driveway, I couldn't help but visualize the pathetic figure I had seen earlier in the evening and think how far the mighty can fall.

My thoughts were interrupted when we arrived at the

front of the house. The teak double doors were flung open to reveal the woman who had been with Tom McCloskey at the Admiral Risty restaurant. I didn't hear what Bilbo said, but I saw him thrust the search warrant in her face and brush her aside as he entered the house in advance of Chief Wilson and three of Palos Verdes' finest.

When I entered the massive foyer, I didn't have a chance to admire the paintings hanging on the walls. Instead, Bilbo demanded that I lead the way.

I looked around the room to find the woman. I saw her in a spirited conversation with Chief Wilson. She was right in his face, yelling and cursing, with arms swinging in every direction. I hated to interrupt the tirade. It's not often that I hear a police chief getting his butt chewed out. I think Bilbo shared my sentiments because, when I glanced over at him, I could see him staring at the two with a barely distinguishable smile on his face.

When I got beside the woman, she quieted down for a moment and said in a voice of pure venom, "Yes."

I told her to show me to Mr. Jung's study. I could tell by the change of her facial expression that I had thrown her off balance. I gave her another emotional whack in the face when I addressed her as Miss Ching, her real name.

Her eyes widened and her mouth dropped open. She turned on her heels and said tersely, "Follow me."

Following her down the hall and up a flight of stairs wasn't exactly a chore. This woman made Susan Wong, who was beautiful even in death, look like a chambermaid. She had more curves under her black-laced robe than San Francisco's Lombard Street, which is billed as the crookedest street in the world. Watching the rhythmic swing of her hips as she went up the stairs made me think that, if they arrested her, I'd volunteer to have her paroled in my custody.

At the top of the steps, she had to wait for the middle-aged men to catch up and then proceeded down a long hallway. It was like a corridor in a major hotel with doors on either side. Several doors cracked open with faces peering out.

I turned and said, "There must be dozens of people here."

The woman replied, "There are eighteen people living here, if you must know. This floor is for family only. There are twelve family members. The servants live on the ground floor in another wing."

"And which part of the house do you live in?" I inquired.

By that time, we were at the end of the hall. She pointed to a door at the right. "That is my room."

"And where is Mr. Jung's room?"

"It is there." She pointed to the door at the end of the hall. "Next to mine."

Bilbo said, "And I'll bet the rooms are adjoining."

She ignored the remark and pointed to the doorway directly in front of us. "There is the study. It is locked and I don't have a key."

Bilbo pushed his way forward. "Do you know where a key is? Otherwise we are going to have to bust the door down."

She turned toward Jung's bedroom door. "I'll get the key."

Bilbo motioned to one of the uniformed officers to follow.

When Wilson had caught up to us, Bilbo told him that

she was getting a key to the study, and further remarked, "You noticed that she hasn't asked where Jung is?"

"How did they grab this guy?" asked Wilson.

"I have no idea. I couldn't tell you what he was wearing. He could have had pajamas on for all I know."

While we were talking, we heard movement in the study. The door opened and we went in.

Once inside, I stopped to get my bearings. When the Triad Chief had told me where his safe was, he hadn't been very coherent. He'd said that it was behind the bookcase.

Behind a table, similar to the one in the travel office, was a wall-to-wall, built-in bookcase. I pointed to the bookcase and said, "We're looking for a safe behind that bookcase."

Bilbo ordered his uniforms to take a look.

The efficient officers located the safe behind the books within minutes.

The woman cried out, "You can't go in there." She tried to grab one of the officer's arms.

The other officer grabbed her from behind and wrestled her away.

Bilbo yelled, "Get her out of here, but don't take her far."

She was led away, screaming that she didn't know the combination.

The officer who found the safe, swung the door open, "It's not latched."

Bilbo, Wilson, Bill and I all moved around the table to the safe at the same time.

"Look for a picture," I told them. "He told me that all I needed to see was a picture."

We all deferred to Chief Wilson who pulled out several

eight and a half by eleven brown manila envelopes one by one, handing them back to Bilbo.

When the safe was empty, Bilbo took them over to the table and examined their contents.

We found what we were looking for in the third envelope—a Polaroid picture of McCloskey holding a jar containing his dead wife's ear and the poodle's ear.

Wilson said to me, "You do good work. We owe you. This will pretty well wrap up this case." He told Bilbo to go pick him up.

Bilbo was ready to leave when I said, "Got a favor to ask you."

"Name it."

Before answering Bilbo, I turned to Bill and asked, "How long it will take to get an edition on the street?"

Bill said, " We can be on the street by six."

"You heard the man," I said to Bilbo. "Give us until six before you give this to anyone else."

From behind me, Wilson said, "Get going. You got it. If we find anything more after we search the rest of the place, we'll let you know."

"Call us at the *Digest* office," Bill yelled over his shoulder as we dashed out of the study and headed for our car.

While Bill was calling his staff, I started writing the ending to a wild couple of weeks.

PALOS VERDES ESTATES
POLICE ARREST HUSBAND
IN ASIAN WOMAN'S
SLAYING

Early this morning, Palos Verdes

Estates Police, led by Detective Rodney Bilbo, arrested Tom McCloskey, husband of slain Susan Wong-McCloskey for her brutal slaying two weeks ago. McCloskey is accused of hiring a hit man from one of the local Triad gangs operating in the South Bay.

It took me over an hour to finish. Bill took another half-hour to proof it. By the time we had concluded, we had enough for a full page. It was quite a night's work.

EPILOG

The special edition of the *Peninsula Digest* hit the streets with a resounding bang. The local public devoured every word. Most people said, "I knew it was him all along." For the second time since we started coverage, the wire services and the local television media picked up the paper's story. By the morning of the second day, it was relegated to a blurb in the mainstream press. By that afternoon, it had been replaced by the latest sex allegation in the nation's capitol.

Of all the people I'd worked with on this case, the most interesting had been Carleton Yang. I called him a wily old bastard when I left his office for the last time. I said that because the picture I saw behind his desk was of a young man in a cap and gown at a university graduation ceremony, inscribed to "dear uncle." The picture was of our friend, Special Agent Sun Fu Yee.

As soon as I'd seen that, I had known I'd been set up. When I'd talked with Sun Fu Yee later, he admitted that his uncle had arranged the office bugging for my benefit so I would make demands. This would force him to intercede with the Hong Kong detectives on my behalf to get the information I needed.

Why did he have to go to such lengths? Simple. The

Elders had wanted to stonewall me because of what I had written earlier. The meeting I'd listened in on had had an agenda meant for my ears. Carleton Yang couldn't lie to them and work with me against their wishes. He was too honorable for that, so he'd had to find a way where they'd have no choice.

The empty office we had been in was leased by Yang, so it had been a simple thing for his nephew to transfer the equipment from an actual tap that had just been concluded to set up the charade.

One enormous tragedy was that Sidney Lu had become an innocent victim. His digging for facts had led to his death. The Triad had ordered it, strangely enough, because they didn't want to be attached to the illegal Democratic National Committee campaign contribution investigation.

No one ever found out who the mysterious "L" was in Susan Wong's appointment book. I have to admit that I had some nagging thoughts about who it might have been, and if my meeting with Lucinda had been accidental. Fearing the worst, and not wanting to know, I never asked her.

I headed back to Chicago, but fully intended to take Bill up on his offer and relocate back to Southern California. The weather is great, and Lucinda is still available and willing.

I was going back to quit my job, and hoped I could make a living freelancing. I haven't made that move yet, but I have made up my mind that I'm going to adopt a healthier lifestyle, or my name isn't Jeremy Dawkins.

The End